The Key Club

This is Dedicated to Glenn.

Also known as Fluffy.

A man Larger than Life itself.

Not just in stature, but Heart as well.

Prologue:

When the ladies started having what the locals believed to be the flu bug, it became a surprise. As pregnancies are found, the experiment unfolds. "Birthing's will have to be announced." "How will this discovery effect the children of the town?" "Plans have started to come to light!"

Welcome back to The Key Club.

Where the question "Who's your daddy?" comes with a whole new meaning.

As Dr. Halloway's waiting room filled with female patients. The flu is making its way through town. But Dale Halloway had other concerns. *What if teenagers decide following the key club's steps for procreation.* With the town's population dwindling, Dr. Halloway did some rough computations. Shaking his head, Dale Halloway knew this would need to happen for a minimum of 20 years or more. This would bring up the census numbers. Judge Harold's plan will be the blueprint for the other towns to do the same.

Making Notes for later charting, nurse Kelly was instructed to do both a blood drawing and a urine analysis. Both are designed to differentiate between pregnancy and illness. As the waiting room clears out, the ladies left with cold meds to start, as the blood work would come back after a few days. Then After the results came back, he would speak with Judge Harold.

Closing the office, Dale felt a cold breeze. "I know dad, you do not approve of my medical practice, but truthfully there seemed to be no other alternative; our town will die. I know you had issues with Judge Harold over Hildi's illness. But dad, I know you love Hildi also. Your anger about mom's death, it wasn't Judge Harold's fault. You signed her death certificate knowing the truth would destroy her memory in the eyes of our fair town. She was in so much pain; the drink was to ease the pain and float away peacefully. It eats Judge Harold's soul; he just wanted Hildi to be out of pain. His arrogance will be what either saves or kills this town."

As Dale locks the office door, he feels a warm breeze flowing through him. "Yes mom, I know dad always loved you. I love you mom, good night." Walking through the town as the snow glistened against a pitch-black sky. The cold turned the night sky into a vastly lit design of brightly lit stars. Opening the door, Dale immediately started a fire in the living area.

Checking out the furnace, Dale knew it would take at least an hour before the chill came out of the air. Plugging in his heated blanket, heading to the kitchen, Dale warmed up potato soup and a brandy before he retired for the night. Walking through the dining room, he noticed the answering machine light blinking. As Dale listened, the lab had some confusing results with the blood drawings?

Turning off the machine Dale shrugs, "I'll contact them in the morning." Blowing on his soup, Dale took a large bite, swallowing the liquid warmed his chest and spread downward from there.

Enjoying the warmth of the soup, he knew things were about to change for better or worse. Judge Harold's plan was in full swing. After consuming his bedtime brandy, Dr. Halloway turned in for th3e night.

As the sun began to rise, "Dr. Halloway it's time to rise and shine sir. Breakfast in 20 minutes, here's some coffee to start with Sir." Thinking for a moment Dale asked, "Where's Millie?"

"Millie Finally had her baby, she had a hard labor, so she will be in the hospital for a little while." "Why didn't she ask for me to deliver?" "She felt you had much on your plate." "Millie is always so thoughtful. You tell her I will still pay her maternity leave. She should not have to worry about money." As mini-Sue spoke, she showed the reverence & respect once given to his parents. Mini explained, "We know you care about ***all*** the towns people." Dale smiled, saying, "You are my friends as well as my patients or employees. So, you're apart of me."

"You need to shake it up, Sir. Also, Nurse Kelly has already called for you."

"They can wait; I'm going to enjoy my beautiful breakfast you've made for me." Taking time to enjoy his meal, thoughts go to how this town can make you feel needed, but alone at the same time. As Doc. Halloway bundled up, turning up his collar, and covering his ears, he trudged through the snow. With fingers crossed, his truck would be ready. "This walking is for the birds." The closer Doc. Halloway got to his office, he discovered he wasn't alone. Both Nurse Kelly and Judge Harold were waiting for him.

"It's a little early for you isn't it Judge Harold?" "Well, did you hear from the lab?" "Yes, they left a message saying they had concerning results. I believe the lab opens at 8 a.m. So, I will call them in a few minutes. Nurse Kelly," "Yes sir?" "Start the coffee. This could be a long day." After everyone was seated, holding a steaming cup of coffee, he dialed the number for the labs.

Dale Halloway heard the familiar answering service. Once his voice was heard, a familiar voice spoke up. "Hey Dale." "So, what is concerning you?" "The number of positive pregnancy tests for one, and I question the accuracy. That being said, I do know about ***The Key Club***. So, my question is what happens when there are multiple births but not the same father for both children?" Judge Harold questioned, "So you believe that this could be an issue?" "Yes," explained Johnny, "I do. Here is the rub, if they have different partners, one of these ladies could carry two babies by two different fathers at the same time." Scratching his chin, Judge Harold announced, "It should be discussed at the board meeting" "I have verified 3 pregnancies."

"Will the town still raise those children as a community?" "Just remember that multiple births are possible." Thinking a moment of Johnny Blackstone's findings, Judge Harold extends an offer to Johnny to be the official lab Doctor or technician keeping information protected from nosey towns members. "This job comes with a price tag." "If you are referring to my silence, you have it. I'm certain we're going to need more staff." "Check with the local schools, who are doing Nurse training, and a couple of obgyn interns.

I'm suggesting that because they will get credits for graduation with an internship. There's nothing better than having hands-on experience. Plus, a paycheck." "You will have more volunteers than you need!"

"So, how about I put you and Nurse Kelly in charge of procuring more medical staff? You report directly to me and Doc. Halloway." "That sounds reasonable to me." Smiled Johnny. Dale Halloway spoke, "I will be the one to notify the mothers of their bundles of joy, no one else. Hypocritic Oath and all." "Agreed, Doc. So when will you be calling them," asked Judge Harold. "After I read all of the results, because there will be pelvic exams to ascertain they conceived plus possible due dates." "So, you won't tell us," Questioned Judge Harold. "No, I will contact each woman and schedule them appointments. I'll arrange the appointments so they're here at different times. Privacy in this matter is important."

As Judge Harold headed to the town hall, there's almost a skip in his footsteps. Thinking out loud he says, "Hildi, it's working!" Duwanna gave her usual greeting. Harold told her, "I need you to set up another board meeting for Wednesday evening and it's mandatory." "Yes Sir! Is there anything good to report?" "That's yet to be determined." Wrinkling up her nose, she knew Judge Harold was hiding information. Duwanna knew if anyone could find out what the Judge was hiding; Lilly would be the one.

"Judge Harold, heading out to get your green tea." "Pick me up a muffin or bagel, I'm starving." Duwanna headed for the local coffee shop. She put in an order for the judge. "A spinach & tomato omelet with whole wheat toast, light butter, a small juice, and green tea."

Smiling at Duwanna, Lilly asked, "For our friend Judge Harold?" "Yes, but he is acting like a little kid with a secret. Demanding a mandatory Wednesday night board meeting attendance." "Interesting," Lilly smiled, "Who got his shorts in a bunch already this morning?" "I don't know, but this is not his normal self." "Ahhh, I understand now," Lilly knew she would need to physically see him. He couldn't lie to Lilly.

As Lilly walked back to the beauty salon, she began to plan her evening meal with Harold. Calling Janet, Lilly assumed she could enlighten her. To Lilly's surprise, it wasn't Janet who answered the phone. "The home of Judge Harold how may I help you?" "With whom am I speaking?" "Mimi Sue Ma'am. Miss Milly had her baby, so I am her replacement." "So where is Janet?" "Oh, she is doing the grocery shopping and other errands." "Ok, please ask her to call Lilly as soon as she returns." "Yes Ma'am." Click.

So many questions, thought Lilly. "I guess I will have to use my charms to get the information." Her voice had a cackle to it as she spoke out loud to herself. There was a twinkle in her eye as she thought; *the game is afoot.* As Doc Halloway studied the blood cultures of his patients, he began making phone calls. Three pregnancies will be difficult without staff.

Doc made appointments for a couple of hours between each patient. Leaving enough time between each patient is important. He started with Lisa, the principal's wife. Her appointment was at 10a.m. then Judith at 1 P.m., and Roz at 4 p.m. With each visit Doc Halloway gave the happy news, or so he thought.

Lisa was excited as she and Lawrence had been trying for a year. So, it will be an August baby. Judith Summers was less than impressed; her career had started to take off, and it would be desk duty again! But she also was due to have hers in the summer. Roz did have a flu bug but was also pregnant and due September 1st. She knew it would be a long, hot summer.

Judith had asked about options. "I will have to mention it to Judge Harold." Once news of pregnancies was whispered throughout the town Reverend Thomas became angry and disheartened. Why wasn't he part of planning these births? The auxiliary will have a field day with this news!

As new of the mandatory board meeting spread through town, members of the auxiliary began whispers of sexually transmitted diseases because of mixing breeding with unapproved people. *Bloodlines are to be pure, not mixed, because inferior people will believe they are one of us. That is not acceptable.*

This will teach our children that they are equal and that can never be allowed! As Bernadine, Silvia, Lucilla discussed how this could ruin their auxiliary. Silvia announced, "We are the elite in our town! So, this must be stopped."

Reverend Thomas stood outside the rectory doors listening to the women conspiring to keep the towns lineage pure. "They're going to need me to help keep the spirituality of our town alive." Sparks of ideas for sermons ignited his heart and mind. Heading to his office Reverend Thomas began writing about sin, the towns *people need to know that there are* ***moral*** *ways of keeping our town alive*.

Even though the auxiliary doesn't approve, the consequences of judging the town's people could cause bigger problems. As he feverishly wrote his sermon, he felt like he was being watched. Shaking it off Reverend Thomas checked the time. School will be letting out soon and talks about a spring pageant that will start with bake sales to help boost fund raising for the senior trip to Florida.

Spring is always busy for the town, but 1st the Valentines party for the adults with Lilly at the helm. It will be a fun event. As Lilly listens to Janet, she knows exactly how to set up the mood to find out why Harold called a meeting. The word mandatory rang in her ears.

This meal will be gumbo, salad, and thick sliced garlic bread for scooping up the gravy served over rice, and a side of red beans for extra protein. She added a small Brandy, decaf coffee, with custard pie for dessert. Smiling Lilly whispers, “You have to feed all the man's appetites." Some things Lilly knew all too well.

In the meantime, Lisa, Judith, and Roz were planning on how to announce this to their prospective families.

As Lawrence came home, Lisa ran to him excitedly as a small child when receiving a small toy. "So, what's got you all excited?" "It's finally happened Lawrence, we're pregnant!"

Somewhere between excited and horrified Lawrence coughed out, "I'm happy too Lisa!" After Lisa headed off to bed Lawrence began to wonder if he was really a daddy. Concerns plagued his dreams. As Lawrence made coffee at 4 a.m. he also wondered who else got the same news.

Roz explained her news to Frank. "Well let's not tell the kids until we must, just in case there's a problem. We aren't young anymore Roz." "It's taken years to get rid of my last round of baby fat."

Judith woke Jack up earlier than normal so she could share her news. As it really started to dawn on Jack he asked, "Did you ask Doc Halloway about options?" "Yes, it wasn't received well." "Well Jude, in for a penny," "I know in for a pound." "What about telling the kids?" Judith exclaimed, "Not yet!"

As Lilly predicted, Harold told all. "So, the board meeting is to announce it?" "We have those nosey auxiliary broads; they will cause problems." "I also think there will be dissention in the ranks." "Jealousy? Or why me?" "Exactly Lilly!" "I will be there with bells on Harold. You know I will always support your decisions."

"I need to open the school early, a little tutoring on color and tint class." Truth be told, a student took on a client outside of class and now Lilly must fix the mess! Before the arrival of the outside client, Lilly took her student to task.

"If you wanted to take a client, it should have been done here under *my* supervision! So, as a lesson, you will clean every station. Top to bottom at the end of class for the next two weeks. Our cleaning service will get to have a two-week vacation on you! Do you understand me?" "Yes ma'am."

Lilly pretended to be angry, but truth be told it happens often at her school. Kids just get ahead of themselves; it happens every semester. High schoolers tend to be a little arrogant and self-assured. Sometimes a reality check is needed. At 7 a.m. sharp the color victim arrived. Lilly greeted her warmly, "Ok, pull off the head scarf and let's have a look at the damage." Swallowing hard, Lilly lifted the scarf to find bubblegum pink hair. "Well, I suppose it could be worse. So, we'll start with stripping the color out and heavy conditioning."

After 4 conditioning treatments, they decided on a deep maroon color. Both to color and highlight her natural red highlights. Once again, Lilly saved the day and her student's neck. All while highlighting the students' mistakes in her class. The Student, Claira Asked, "When do I get to color again?"

Looking gently into Claira's eyes, Lilly says, "Once you learn not to mess up our mannequin's hair" After her harsh tone, Lilly spoke softly to Claira, "Honey you aren't the 1st student to mess up hair tinting class. It's the lesson you learn from it that matters." Giving Claira a hug, Lilly whispers, "Go fix your face, mascara is running down your face." After a good cry, Claira emerged from the restroom full of vigor, ready to try again.

Students had questions about the "Key Club" and its true purpose. Lilly carefully suggested that parents should be asked these questions. Walking back to the Salon, Lilly knew things were about to break loose. With the pregnancies starting already, guidelines needed to be revamped to include the new arrivals.

As thoughts began to swirl, Lilly walked into slow traffic, not paying attention. A few locals asked her if she was practicing her red-carpet walk. "No, it already takes way too much work to get a man's attention!" "Miss Lilly, you know we would gladly give you all the attention you need."

Laughing heartily, Lilly smiles, "Bet you sling that bullshit at your wives too! Have a nice day Gentlemen." Shaking her head. "These boys have been chasing my tail for years. They haven't caught me yet. Now, I need to open the shop." As clients drifted in the talk began, speculation on the board meeting.

Roz was feeling under the weather between the flu and pregnancy. She was green faced and puking. “Mom, you look like crap,” “Thanks a lot,” With all the bravado of the oldest child, “Mom just go to bed, we will make dinner.” “Sure, you will. Just order pizza.” Laughing loudly Kal said, “It's food you don't have to cook!” “Ok, you win, you're in charge tonight. Don't forget homework and baths tonight. Check your brothers' ears, I think he has a potato patch growing in there!”

“Here mom, you get in bed, I will run get you soup and ginger ale!” “You are such a grown-up young man. No increase in allowances until report cards are out though.” “Deal mom!” “Now please get me some ginger ale.”

Heading out Kal tells the others he's in charge, “Pizza for dinner tonight, but homework & baths." "Aw come on man, now you sound like the grown-ups." "If we get everything done, we will watch a movie, fair?" "Guess we don't get a choice."

"Mom is sick with the flu, so don't bother her. Behave I will be right back, gotta put the pizza order in, and get ma some soup for her tummy." 20 minutes later, Kal came back. "Pizza, salad, and bread sticks on their way. Homework done?" "Almost, math is hard." "Ok, I will help, just let me take this to mom 1st." Frank arrived to discover the kids eating and doing homework. Pinching himself, Frank yelled, "No! I'm not dreaming!"

"Dad, I got the antipasti salad you like." "Who are you and what have you done with Kal?" "Relax dad, mom is sick, so I'm in charge." "Ok, I'm starved," smiled Frank. As the children finished, they were sent to take their baths. "Dad, I can't find my favorite shirt!" "Let me check with mom." "She's sound asleep." Frank headed for the laundry room. Folded neatly was the shirt in question, smiling frank whispers, "She always knows." Tucking his siblings into bed, little Rose Marie asked, "Kal is momma going to die?" "No, she just has the flu." "Eeew puking is yucky." "Just let mom rest ok, good night."

Frank decided to attend the board meeting. Judge Harold brought the meeting to order. "As you may have heard, we have three confirmed pregnancies. We also may face multiple pregnancies. This is because of our club meetings."

Smiling Lilly explains, "There's a possibility of 2 babies with separate dads or it could belong to husbands, so we apply the rules we started with. All children are raised in a communal environment."

"No one discusses their lineage or other personal information. We all signed on for this to save our town, and you are free to move if these rules offend you." Judge Harold looks at everyone pointedly. Lilly shifts the direction again, "Alright, now to plan our next event!" She never missed a beat as she smiled, "With Valentine's Day coming I believe ***treats*** should be available." Frank spoke up, "Maybe another costume party?" "Ok! God, I expect five ideas from each of you!" "This meeting is adjourned.

Writing down ideas, putting them in a bowl *"So everyone's ideas get heard"*, and driving home. Frank thought about talking to his oldest son about the true meaning for the ***"Key Club"***, but would he understand or would he hate his parents for dragging the family into this?

"Ung, I'm sure Reverend Thomas would have many things to say, the least of which would've been being asked. Leering at the younger girls, hoping a girl would show him some attention. He truly creeps me out." Thought Frank.

Stopping at the bowling alley, Frank made sure it was locked up for the night. Grabbing a couple of 20's out of the safe. Frank would pay Kal some extra for helping his mom. Kal was a good kid, who will do well in college. This pleases Frank and Roz. Neither will have the chance at an advanced education; Kal will be the 1st to attend college. Slipping through the house quietly, Frank noticed Kal fell asleep studying.

Gently waking him for bed, Frank slips 2 twenties into his shirt pocket. "I'm proud of you son." Trudging up the stairs, Kal falls, face first, on his bed. The sound of soft snoring filled the air.

Overnight, a soft, accumulative blanket of snow covered the ground. The sound of state guys could be heard plowing the roads. "Looks like a snow day coming, better open the alley." As the news announced cancellations and delays, the children cheered with Glee.

Roz slowly navigated the stairs, "Why aren't you ready for school?" in unison the children piped, "Snow Day!" A wave of nausea hit Roz. All she could do was run for the kitchen sink. Little Rose Marie scrunches her nose, yelling, "Eeew yucky! Mommy you are sick, go to your room!" Shaking her head, Roz realized her baby girl knew mommy needed to be in bed.

"Kal, maybe we should call nurse Kelly." "She has medicine that tastes like bubblegum!" Little Rose chimed in. Thinking for a moment Kal called Nurse Kelly. Putting Rose Marie on, she explained, "Mom is sick and needs your bubblegum medicine." With a soft chuckle Nurse Kelly said, "Okay." Handing the phone to Kal, Nurse Kelly asked, "Your mom is still feeling bad? I will have Dr. Halloway write a script for nausea." "Thanks, I tried doing mom's job it's harder than it looks." Nurse Kelly says, "I understand."

Doc Halloway listened to the call, "One nausea script coming right up! Let's try coke syrup to settle her stomach. That way if someone decides to taste it, it's no problem safe for all. The fact that Kal took over for his mom shows he's willing to help."

"If all the teenagers accept new roles in the family, it could make for an easier transition."

As Doc Halloway called in the prescription, he spoke to Donald, the local pharmacist, or Dr. D as the kids called him. “Hay Dale, I usually speak with Nurse Kelly.” “Sorry to disappoint Don, but I need you to keep a healthy supply of Coke syrup on hand.” “What the flu already?” Bitched Dr. Don. “Seems upset tummies will run through the town like wildfire.” “Seems about right, So who's this coke syrup for?” “Roz,” Doc Halloway says, “Is she ok?” “Yes, her youngest called the office for bubblegum medicine for her mom.” Smiling, Dr. Don understood where the little one was coming from.

"You know, I think we should start doing school field trips again so they can learn about new careers.” “Sure, sounds like a fun project for the kids. Cartain jobs are for college born kids, and some are AG or tech education. More subjects to talk about at the board meetings.” “I better get this to Roz, so her kids feel more at ease.”

A knock at the door signaled Rose Marie to answer the door. "Hi, Dr. Halloway, Mommy is upstairs in bed; she is sick. Kal is making her toast with tea, and I'm reading her stories!" "It sounds like your mom is in good hands then." Doc Halloway smiles and little Rose Marie. "We try but hers puking." Says Rose Marie as they round the corner to Roz's room. She expressed her undying gratitude for giving her something that helped. Roz explains, "It's never hit me like this before." "With age it does seem more difficult." "Will the other ladies have these issues?" Thinking about the other ladies who tested positive.

"Judith Summers doesn't seem to want to practice what was discussed. So, this will also be a part of the new board meeting." "Valentine's weekend should be fun. It's not a religious holiday, so no one can complain. I'm sure Miss Lilly will have many treats for the party."

Lisa asked Lawrence, "Now that we are pregnant, should we still go to the club meetings?" Thinking a moment he said, "That's a good question." "Should we ***guess*** about who is pregnant?" "We're expected not to discuss it until their families have been told," Lawrence says, "Yes, that would be the right thing to do." "I think Judith might be, cause she's looking tired and disheveled. However, the flu is still bouncing around town, and it happens every year." "Along with spring colds and allergy season." Lawrence chimed in.

"We also have 4 more months until high school graduation." "Boy, I hope Judge Harold has a plan on how to handle this, or it could get messy." "So, are you going to be up for attending the board meeting?" "Of course, pregnancy is no excuse not to attend." Doc Halloway looked at Roz, feeling her discomfort regarding throwing up. This also caused concern for the ladies testing positively. Would the others have a difficult 1st trimester? He began making mental notes as he walked back toward the office.

Nurse Kelly greeted him with, "Your wheels are ready for pickup." "Great now I won't have to walk in subzero temperatures in the morning."

As Doc Halloway walked to the garage, he felt an eye staring at him. Turning around to the right, he noticed a slightly familiar car following him.

Dale was called out. As he turned, Duwanna honked her horn. "Oh Duwanna, did you need something?" Dale asked. "Halloway? Is it Judge Harold?" "Sort of?" With a questioning look, Dale said, "Let's go have coffee." Knowing it might be about the club, he felt certain it should be a private conversation.

Duwanna waited for Doc Halloway to pick up his wheels before heading to the Comfort Coffee house. As the waitress took orders, Duwanna started to relax a bit. After being served, Duwanna asked, "What do you know about Judge Harold's brother?" "Not much." Said Dale, "Why?" "It seems he has been released from the correctional facility?"

Thinking a moment before he spoke, "They called him Fluffy because of his large status. He rode with a biker club. He protected a woman from the wrath of his brothers in the Club. There was an altercation, and it was brutal. His brother was killed by his own hand. So, he was charged with voluntary manslaughter and received 8 years. Even though his intentions were to protect, someone died by his hands. There were conveniently guns and drugs found at his apartment, but they were proven not to be his. However, his so-called brothers wanted him to pay for going against his brotherhood."

Doc Halloway began to ponder how this would affect the "Key Club". Will Fluffy come back to town? Memories started flooding back to Judge Harold and his brother.

"They had a healthy rivalry, no matter if it was sports, girls, or jobs. Their fights were famous around town. At one point they got into it over Miss Hildi, but as we all know, the Judge won the ultimate lady."

Duwanna spoke, "I guess that was the way before my family arrived here. So, does that mean he will come back here?" "Well, for a facility to release an inmate, they normally try to establish a place of residence to release them to." "So, you think the Judge knows?" asked Duwanna.

"I'm sure he's had contact with the warden. Will he return home? I won't know until I speak with Harold." "Well maybe the Judge will let him stay in the family home until he finds a job." Dale shakes his head, "There are some old wounds there that may not have healed, and the Judge ***never*** forgets." "Ah, even though they are brothers, they are still rivals."

Millie came in for breakfast to go. Questioning this action, Duwanna called her over to their table. "What's going on?" "The Judge isn't coming to the office today." Doc Halloway asked, "Is Harold not feeling well?" "That's putting it mildly. Seems he will be having a live in guest for a while, so there's the whole house to clean and groceries to buy." Duwanna looked at both, "I guess he knows!" Millie's look said she was clearly confused. "Seems the Judges brother is being released from a facility." "Like prison?" Millie asked.

"I believe so," said Duwanna. Figuring Millie would need an explanation, "The short version is that he was a part of a biker club who intended to severely hurt a woman.

He intervened on her behalf. His brethren didn't accept it. Women are less then important in their view. There were an altercation and the man died. They planted guns and drugs in his place."

"When all was said and done, he did 8 years for voluntary manslaughter. Even though it was done to protect another, he had to be sentenced because the man died." Millie nodded, "Ok, I understand now, he was trying to protect." "Yes, and it went very wrong." "This explains the Judges mood swings."

Leaving with a bag of food for Judge Harold, she now understood. With her head down, Millie ran smack into Lilly. "Oh gosh! I'm so sorry!" Millie squawked. "Why are you apologizing to me, Millie? We are equals."

"Thank you, ma'am." Shaking her head Millie knew that even though she was equal in Miss Lilly's view, not everyone would agree. Thinking about those snotty auxiliary broads she knew they made women like Millie feel inferior, it made them feel superior. Lilly smiled as she thought those pristine closets had many skeletons.

"So, what's up Doc?" "Seems the Judge isn't coming into the office today. He's having company." "No company, Just Reggie. Fluffy will be here for a while." "So, no one told us?" whined Dale.

"Truthfully, he wasn't sure he was going to allow him to return home. However, after speaking with the Warden, Harold reconsidered. His brother has been a model inmate; he was promoted to trustee. After reviewing the court records, he understood that he protected his woman and his club brother died.

It was no other reason. Warden fully admitted they didn't want to sentence him, but when there's a death there need to be punishment, and 8 years was the minimum." Lilly knew that it would help them work through their past issues. "So will Harold tell him about the Key Club?" "If he doesn't someone else will!" "Millie will fix up his old room." "Do you know him?" Lilly asked Duwanna. "Yes, we all attended school together."

"So, what's your take on it?" "Reggie, Fluffy rather, was a very handsome man. Athletic and very smart. He wasn't good at sitting down. He joined the biker club after Hildi passed away. It seems Harold and Fluffy were at odds when it came to her health. Harold knew it would be very painful existence, so he did as she asked and let her go.

Fluffy would have robbed a bank to keep her in treatment, he leaned a lot on Hilda when his parents passed. Almost like a mom, she could always keep the peace between the brothers." "So, who else knows about his arrival Lilly?" "I'm not sure because he was not sure he wanted his brother to come back home."

With a sad smile, Lilly explained. "I believe. The judge needed reassurance that he wasn't a murdering son of a bitch. Once he reviewed all the evidence, he even contacted witnesses or witness protection to arrange to speak with the victim via phone. He needed to be sure his brother's intentions were decent, and he wasn't caught with his pants down, so to speak, but after speaking with her, she explained what kind of torture she would endure until she finally died."

"Her handlers showed Harold pictures of what happened to the last girl that they were displeased with. That answered any motive or questions Harold had." "She then said they should have given him a metal for killing that pig. Harold Knew it was done for the protection of others, just like a good soldier would do. Knowing The truth gave him. Answers needed for the decision."

"So, when does he arrive?" Asked Doc Halloway. "Harold will pick him up tomorrow and bring him home." "I will assume Millie will be very busy today," smiled Dewanna as she paid the check.

Lilly explained. "I put one of my senior cosmetologists in charge of the class so I can be of assistance to Millie." Understanding Doc asked about the board meeting, "As far as I know it continues as scheduled."

Lilly tells the waitress, "I'm here to pick up soup for Roz. She has a tummy bug." Looking to the waitress. "Extra crackers please." Doc asked. "Still?" "Yes, the coke syrup helps but, she is very weak so chicken soup." Smiling Doc says, "I see you have everything in hand." "Yes, Doctor. I will be checking in on all our flu patients."

Dewanna headed back to the office to manage the judge's calendar, cackling as she drove back to the office. "This should lighten up the town's board meeting up. The gossip Queens and Reverend Thomas will turn this into a bitch fest."

Dropping in on Roz, Lilly announced herself as Little Rose Marie appeared. “My mommy is sick. She barfs all the time. So, I made her toast.” “You're such a good nurse.” Lilly smiled. “Is that for Mommy?” “Yes, it is.” “OK!” “And here's some chocolate for you, because it's a hard work being a nurse.”

“Kal Miss Lilly has soup for Mommy.” With a slight smile, he greeted Lilly. “It's hard doing a mom's job.” “Well, I will stay for a while, why don’t you go on to the bowling alley for a while.” “Are you sure?” “I will make sure everything is taken care of. Naps will be needed soon anyway.” Looking a bit haggard, he nods and heads out, trudging through the accumulated snow drifts. He'd be glad when spring was here.

Warming up the soup, Lilly set up a tray for Roz. With the sleeve of crackers, and a glass of ginger ale. Lilly, heads upstairs. Rose Marie announced that Lilly brought soup with a faint smile. Roz mouthed. ***Thank you***. "So, how's it going?" "We decided to wait until I am through the 1st trimester before announcing it, just in case. I'm not a spring chicken anymore."

Lilly giggled, "I don't believe you are ready to be put out to pasture." Little Rose Marie announced, "My mommy is not an old cow." "No, dear, she is not." Climbing up in momma's bed, Lilly was getting the old stink eye. Lilly chatted for a few minutes when Roz started to snore a bit. Lilly whispers. "I will let the two of you nap a while."

Taking her tray to the kitchen, Lilly headed to the home of Judge Harold. Upon her arrival, she noticed rooms pulled apart and polished to perfection. "So, what bring what brings you out here, Lilly?" "Thought you could use a couple extra hands." Nodding, Harold knew she was truly there for moral support. She remembered how it had been in high school. As Lilly walked through each room feelings and memories came flooding in.

A warm blush covered her body. "Those were some of the best times." "A penny for those flushed thoughts, Lilly." "I have fond memories of this house which both your parents and Hildi. Even though your family had money the house was open to all. None of that BS you tend to see and hear from most in the in this town." With a smile, Harold puts a strong arm around Lilly's shoulders. "Here I found this in a box of pictures."

Looking at an old black and white picture with Hildi, Lilly, Fluffy, and the rest of the graduating class. "I remember that. Families couldn't afford to throw graduation parties. Your dad took the podium announcing graduation festivities would be at their home for all the kids, even if they weren't graduating. Come over. They were so good to everyone." Lilly smiled. "Your parents helped but never gloated."

"My sisters magically found new dresses for the holidays. My brothers usually got bikes from your dad. I remember your dad trying out the sled and broke his arm." "But he was right back out there with them." "I think that's why I celebrate the town's Christmas the way I do, because of all the love your parents showed all of the kids."

"I found our Prom pictures too." "Ohh Harold, Hildi was so beautiful! You looked great except Fluffy took up most of the picture." Lilly laughed. "Reggie was like a one-man defense line. He was unstoppable. That's why those pros. checked him out, he just willing to follow a different path." "Well, headstrong is a family trait." Lilly Laughing hard.

Harold said, "It helps in the legal arena, yes." "Think about how much money your mom could raise for a worthy cause." "Roz and Judith were cheerleaders and on the debate team. We truly had a great high school back in the day." "None of the guys were a slouch either," smiled Lilly. "Jeez. We have been gabbing instead of working."

"Millie has done a wonderful job on short notice, but I went to see Roz today and she looks really green around the gills." "From what I understand it's normal." "Harold, Judith is looking for options. So how is this going to be handled?" "She was a part of the plan since its inception, the rule applies to everyone in the Key Club."

"Lisa's all excited because they had been trying." "Well, at least one mom to be is happy about being pregnant." "So next issue. Do you tell your brother? Because Reverend Thomas and all the auxiliaries would be happy to explain our lack of morals." Thinking a moment, Harold decided, "Let's get him home first, and acclimated to the outside world first, then handle things as they unfold." "That sounds reasonable, Harold. Thank you for being my support always."

"You know how I feel," Millie announced her presence, "Sir. Would you like to inspect his quarters, Sir?" he laughs, "Millie, His quarters will be a mansion compared to where he has been residing." Thinking for a moment, Millie said. "I believe you're correct, Sir. But what about clothing?" "Well, we will have to pick up some, I guess. I haven't seen him in many years. So, size I wouldn't guess at."

"Well. He played football, it was a 3X but he had solid muscle back then." Thinking for a moment, Lilly remembered her brother complaining. "All he had was working out and playing cards, so I'm guessing he would work out quite often." "I need to finish up, so I can go grocery shopping," Lilly commented. "What about your diet?"

"I believe he probably needs this diet. I'm sure they feed them slop because of the sheer amount they must cook and serve. So, it will take a while for his stomach to get used to real food." "I'm sure a real bed will take some getting used to." "Also," Millie looked a little bit confused. "He's been in a facility where they tell you when to eat, sleep, shit, and work." "So, free time will also be unusual for him." Lilly giggled. "Showering alone will also be a new experience for him."

"Maybe they'll call ahead. Maybe you should give him a physical.

There's a strong chance he shares your health issues." "Prison is a pretty solitary place when one is used to riding with other bikers." Lilly nodded. "But Harold, those men might not be very forgiving." "Guards let it slip that he will be in a halfway house in another state, so if they are looking for him, they will have to work to find him.

Warden did say he avoided making friends. Betrayals are normal in that situation. He even had outside work details become easier to come by. Fluffy even earned a degree in social science basics he studied. After culinary pies and comparative Religion. So, he used his time wisely," Millie smiled.

"Yes, there was only one instance in eight years where he was involved in a fight, but again, it was self-defense of a young kid. Once they moved him to a new cell location, he was out of Fluffy's protection."

"He was found dead in a dryer of the laundry area, and your connections won't keep you safe and those places. Our guide became very closed off. Apparently, the guards bet on who would get to that poor kid first. The warden knew but didn't did nothing to prevent it or punish the ones who killed the boy. Records showed it was an accidental death." Judge Harold shook his head with anger then went out to the patio for air. Lilly followed, putting her arms around him for comfort.

Harold explained, "The law has been perverted to accommodate greedy sick men who get off on the torture of other men. Those men don't normally have a means, so they are prostituted for anything of worth, Lilly. If our boy Reggie hadn't been the size of a brick wall I know. He would have met his demise in that place."

"But he's coming home, Harold. We'll be here to help him adjust to small town life again." "So how much does the town board know about his release?" "Nothing yet, but I'm sure the town will know all by sundown."

"What about the Key Club?" "He knows nothing and I would prefer to keep it quiet so he can acclimate to life on the outside." Letting out a sigh, Lilly looked at Harold, reading her thoughts. "Reverend Thomas will relish this news, as well as the Auxiliary."

Laughing hard, Harold cracked a smile. "I think they've met their match." "This will be interesting." Nodded Lilly. "Here Millie, you can drive my car to get the groceries." "Ohh, no Sir, I could never." Lilly smiled. "Would you like me to drive?" "Yes ma'am." Shaking his head, he knew it was a combination of fear and respect from Millie.

Leaving with the list in hand, Millie and Lilly headed out. Harold then called the warden. "I would like to pick up my brother in the evening in case his former club decides to pay him a call." "I have to admit there has been talk by the guards." Growling, his voice got deep and loud. "If a hair is out of place anywhere on his body I will dismantle your prison piece by piece. With some help from senators in Congressman, do you understand me, boy?" "Yes, Sir. I will make sure he is ready. What time will you arrive?" "Do you think I got to the bench by being stupid. No arrival time to keep you on your toes."

Click.

He knew why arrival time was asked. Surprise will keep an equal playing field. The warden was not one for treating inmates equal. He wanted money for his pocket. Sleazy behavior is what the warden was known for. Harold walked through each room. Each filled with memories, touching the mahogany sideboard, his mother kept all her special things. Including her children's school awards.

A smile pressed across his face. As he spies a photograph of both brothers, except for the football Awards. As brothers, they controlled a high coveted scorecard. Both played defense, but their offense worked. They had one full ride for several schools.

Then he found one that made him. Harold full on laugh, his brother stood in full uniform with a cheerleader on his arm. The last in a split between his legs, but gossip is always fun at someone else's expense.

This town has had its fair share of hurting humans because loose lips destroy lives. Strolling upstairs, Harold inspected his brother's room. He displayed proudly pictures from high school. Now to prepare for board meetings and pick up his brother. Harold belts some comfort in having his brother come home and the radio started to play family traditions.

It brought a warm feeling too. Staring off into space, Lilly whispered. "Are you OK?" Shaking his head. "Sorry, lost in my head, in memories." Handing Lilly the picture with a laugh, she spoke." It's amazing that we're still alive. Look how many times I was standing on shoulders." "You have always been beautiful, Lilly." "Look, there's Hildi doing the splits. Here is the other one. You girls hung on us like monkeys." "Those were some great times," writing down notes for the meeting, Lilly cooed.

"Let me run to the board meeting and cover our Valentine's Day event. Harold, go get your brother out of that horrible place." "But how to explain my absence?" "Truth is always best." With a questioning look. "The truth is, you're picking up your brother. Simple." Lilly handing all the pictures to Harold and smiled. "I would say a picture board is in order. It's to remind us of how far we have all come. This is how our town and life together. I will put these in your gifted hands." Lilly kissing Harold's cheek.

"Go get your brother and bring him home." Millie interrupted. "Excuse me Sir, there's some heavy packages." "Oh, I'm sorry. Here, let me get those for you, but only if after this you go home." "But Sir, Your dinner." "I won't be home." "Of course, safe travel, Sir. I am sure you will be happy to see your brother, Sir." "Yes, Millie. It will be good to see him in person." Harold knew Lilly could handle the town board meeting, so things would be done by his rules. But there was still apprehension about bringing his brother home.

The town could be cruel when it came to forgiveness. The town needs to band together, or it won't survive and will be folded into another Township. This is the only alternative, so births are needed to increase the town census. Otherwise, the county will slash the budgets for all the town needs. Shaking his head. He knew he'd better head out.

The well surprise visit pissed off the warden, but it is a necessary evil. Fighters don't forget or accept one of their own killing and members. Assuming there is probably a price on his head which will be which will take a meeting with the President and VP. Harold also knew wheels would need to be greased. In the legal realm, we call it bribery, but it is for the greater good of our town.

As he started to drive, he noticed a beautiful sunset of red folds and a touch of orange. The sky was darkening rather quickly. Pulling into the Wardens personal parking spot, Harold stills himself as to what he might encounter. As he pulls open the door to the Warden's private office, alarms start going off like an air raid.

Guards surrounded Harold like he was an escaped convict. Does Harold laugh? “Easy boys, let me get out my credits in my ID for you.” Instead, they threw him against the wall and patted him down. “Why are you here?” Asked Guard Nielsen. “Well, if you read my identification, you would get it." "I just think you're an asshole here to cause problems." "I see," smiled Judge Harold. "So, I will assume I sentenced a family member, and you felt he received an unfair trial."

As Warden Siemens stood in the darkened hallway, he knew those boys were looking for a fight Judge Harold had passed a sentence of family members so he will not be a popular man here. Warren Seaman announced his presence, "What seems to be the problem?" guard Nielsen asks, "So, what do we do with this piece of shit?" Nodding, Warren Siemens smiled. "He is our guest. Why?" smiling. "He is here to pick up his brother." "What a piece of shit here would have a brother who's a judge?" "Our boy Reggie."

"Reginald Beaufort?" Guard Nielsen replied, "Exactly," smiled Warren Seaman. Walking behind the guards was

Doc Halloway. "Gentlemen, why is he here?" "To make sure said prisoner is an acceptable health for his release." "I see." "So, where's your Infirmary Warden?"

"Guard, please escort Doctor Halloway to our medical area." Upon arrival, Dale noticed it looked like they were preparing for an autopsy. This concerned Dale Halloway deeply. With loud clanking and the turning of keys signaled Fluffy's arrival. As prisoner 9856410 arrived, he stood in silence.

"Step forward, out from the shadow." A very tall man, but he didn't look as he once did. "Reggie, do you Remember Me?" Squinting through blackened eyes, Reggie's voice was hoarse but made a confirmed sound. That hallway was ready for. "Yes, it's me. I need to check you out for release." As he stepped into the light, Dale shook his head.

"I see they threw you a going away party just like a welcome party." they give a list for Scott Halloway to check off for the examine. Halloway was disgusted at the injuries with Manhattan George during his incarceration. Looking at the doctor, he said, "How many? You treat more in this condition more than I can count Fights." "Yes, encouraged by the guards." "So, his mouth is wired shut." It was a statement, not truly a question. "No, that's too compassionate. They make it worse if I question how the inmates." That hurt. "Let me guess, bikers run this place?"

"Not exactly. The man Reggie accidentally killed was kin to our warden and guard, so they sanctioned this treatment. Seems the protection of a woman who spoke up against their president didn't bode well. They thought her daughters would make a nice Layton prize. Our boy didn't agree and the fight was on." "So, am I assuming that that's why Judge Harold got an icy welcome?"

"I took pictures of all his injuries when he came in," slipping them to Halloway for a reference points. "I believe I should escort him to clean out his cell." "No, only guard can be on the block." "Don't think Judge Harold will take that line down." "Well, he can demand it, but I can't guarantee that it will be accepted." Looking at Reggie, "Let's blow this popsicle stand."

Reggie nodded, "Absolutely." Waiting in the Warden's office, Harold looked at his awards, knowing he had paid for them. Doc Halloway returned to the office with a scowl, handing the pictures to Judge Harold as his face turned full on Crimson. "I will be joining your guards to bring this prisoner for his release. And I don't think you can prevent me, Warden. I have jurisdiction." handing him the Supreme Court's ruling.

"Fine," smiled Warden Seaman. "But you need to understand we can't protect you, Sir." With an evil sneer, "I will take my chances Gordon." "Let's go, boys it's past your dinner break." Guards looked at the warden. He nodded, giving permission. Walking through the darkened halls.

As Harold walked, he noticed lights coming up in the cell block along with Doc Halloway. Dale then noticed a man looking like he was having a stroke. With a blood curdling scream, he yelled for guard to open his cell and call for medical now. As the judge watched as the medical team arrived. He knew someone paid for this this man's death.

Warden Seaman condoned his execution. Arriving at his cell, Judge Harold read his paperwork out loud. He was being released, charged through a box of Reggie's stuff. "Hurry up, I'm missing my dinner." As they walked, the guards reminded Reggie he was still their property. He was not free yet. "One slip and you will be ours for life."

Knowing any word from him would be considered a threat, so he stayed quiet. Arriving at Warden Siemens office, he motioned for all to sit, but Reggie knew if he did, it would be considered disrespect and could add time to his sentence. Going through the paperwork the Warden said, "I expect you have learned your lesson," Judge Harold replied with. "You mean his place within the biker community?" "You're running your mouth and I will violate him and he will stay here as our guest."

Understanding, Judge Harold nodded. He controls this world, completing and signing all the forms, removing his shackles from his wrist and ankles. After everything was finished they said goodbye to this hell like facility that Halloway spoke. "This place makes hell seem like a vacation." Pulling out from the parking lot, guards followed till they met a public highway. Turning around, the guards headed back to the prison. Harold suggested they get a bite so he could relax before heading home.

Meanwhile, Lilly was handling the board meeting. "Where's the judge?" "Harold had his own issues to tend to today." "So, we, as the townspeople, aren't worthy of his attention." Lilly begins, seething with anger, showing her picture board his pictures. "I'm sorry I wasn't informed of your royal standing here compared to his family matters. Are you saying that your presence demands his presence more than his own family? Is that what I'm hearing right now?"

"He called the board meeting, didn't he?" "Very well then allow me to recount history. Have a seat." Lilly was seething inside as she looked cooly over the boardroom.

She turned the picture board she had made around for them all to see as she ran her fingers fondly over the pictures. "Incase we've forgotten. We all came from this township. During the football and cheerleaders' pictures, one of our own was wrongly sent to prison because he dared to go against the code to protect women and her daughters. This caused an altercation with club president, at which time he was killed."

"Even though it was done for the protection of others, he served time." Thinking for a moment, Judith was reminded. "Judge Harold went to bring our boy home; he was needed there along with Doc Halloway. So now can we address club business? We have three verified pregnancies so congratulations to our new parents."

"Our Valentine's event will be everything covered. In chocolate, if that is confusing, I have visual aids to help." Reverend Thomas began that everyone is going to hell speech, then brought up what a horrible man Harold's brother was, a felon and not a welcome addition to our town.

Taking a large breath. That made her breasts heave as she spoke, "Really? That's how you wish to start this? Who do you think you are? Reggie was a football star and giving all he could to our town.

The man you were scrutinizing saved the life of a woman and her children from a horribly painful death. He didn't worry about his own well-being."

"Just the safety of these ladies. I never want to hear you, disrespect his good name. He has more honor and decency than any man I've ever encountered. Now go back to your church and pray for your own soul. It needs salvation."

During the meeting, Frank cautiously approached Lilly. "So Fluffy's coming home?" "Yes, but I would imagine it will be difficult to get used to." "Then what about those club members?" "I will pass the word to give him breathing room." "Roz will be happy he's coming home. Those pictures were a nice touch, reminders of why we are fighting to keep our town a live."

Lilly nodded, "I would like to keep our towns people away. It has always been family above all in our town. But you know those snotty auxiliary women will pass judgment pictures containing 1000 words, and trust me, I have some incriminating pictures." "These are Harold's private pictures from his memories."

Frank smiled, "I remember when Fluffy threw me over the goal line because I had the ball and broke my leg. Straight score for the last few minutes of the game." "Finals were a blast too." Laughing, "You were a great quarterback, Frank. Pepper rallies got so loud they put in a noise ordinance. Roz was hot back in the day." Giggled Lilly.

"Homecoming court was great too. Hard to believe you have a son who is preparing for a college tour. Your son had his football in his crib at birth. Damn,

we're old and cranky, aren't we Frank?"
"But we are wise now, right Lilly?"

Laughing hard, Lilly said. "Hardly, but we have learned over the years about the world. Now we are back to protecting our town once again. Goodnight Frank. Stopping at a mom-and-pop place for a much-needed break, Gerald pointed to a booth. In the back was a view of all the doors, just in case.

A waitress came over and asked about drinks, "Coffee, all around," handing out menus she announced, "Let me know when you're ready." Realizing, Reggie couldn't see the menu through swollen eyes and a very painful mouth. Doc Halloway suggested, "Soup and a tuna salad plate for easy consumption." "Sounds good, so the same all around?"

In a half-whispered voice spoke, "You have what you want? I am the one who's a mess, not you guys." As Harold looked through the pictures slipped to Doc Halloway, his wheels were already turning. He would file allegations against warden Seamen and those guards. With an investigation comes sanctions, and new employees. He intended to hurt them in the only way it hurts, the wallet.

"The doc in the infirmary looked as if he was set up for an autopsy?" questioned Halloway. Thinking a moment, Fluffy whispered. "You might have stopped it for this time, but his death will be executed sooner or later. Once you're marked for death, it becomes a contest on who gets you first. I wasn't as easy to push around after a few guards got what was coming to them, I was put in months of solitary and isolation."

"That warden is crooked as an old tree, so now what?" Asked Harold. "Our first order of business is a full workup and getting you healthy," Doc Halloway said. "But the club?" "We haven't heard much on them in a while." "Not on any local court dockets either, so I am not sure if there's still a local charter." Harold noted, "I will look into this," looking into his brother's eyes.

"Good to see you, no matter your condition," smiled Harold. "So where are you gonna hide me at?"Fluffy asked, Harold spoke. "You're coming home where you belong." "Reginald Beauford Harold." "No other place for you, Bud. You're coming Home." "Won't this mess up your perfect Peyton place Town?" laughing hard, "I will bring you up to date after you relax some. Millie prepared your room. Lilly and I found some old pictures from high school. It's a real kick in the pants."

"So how is Miss Lilly?" "Feisty as ever, she keeps our town happy. Drives the snide Broads crazy. The little kids you coached are preparing for college." "Damn, I missed so much." "But you'll be home now." Shaking his head. "I might be putting the townspeople in danger." "Absolutely not. We stand up with our own, No problem, brother." "I hope you're right. I can't do anymore time."

"Warden Seaman deserves a pretty cell of his own, right along with those guards." Harold smiled. "And I will be happy to oblige those needs, as always. Right, Doc?" Laughing hard, Dale says. "You should have seen the attitude I got for trying to put him on a healthy diet for his cholesterol."

"I bet that was quite a challenge." "Not really, He is still not happy. I had to make some adjustments before he'd even try it. 2 cups of coffee per day. Otherwise, herbal tea, less red meat, more veggies, and only two cigars per week. Same with whiskey." "Ohh boy!" "Don't laugh brother. You will be joining me on this diet."

"Hey, it can't be working the slop they fed us in lock up." "Diets bring up a vision of cardboard foods, for fiber. Again," laughter filled the air.

"Let's head out. We need to be careful of the deer running across the road, and I will have to check in with Miss Lilly. She ran the town board meeting." "Ohh, boy. Heads will roll." "True," Harold smiled. "And then, of course, we have Reverend Thomas to deal with." "That treacherous perv is still at our church?" "Yes, he's still there," quietly pulling into the doctor's office.

"See you boys in the morning." Checking his own office for remnants of the board meeting, Fluffy stood in the doorway, looking around as memories flooded his mind. Spotting Lilly's picture board, he touched each picture, when memories had a happier time. Looking at a young man who had the world by the tail.

He felt that he fielded several football offers full ride, but he had plans which never matched those of his parents or his brother. Hildi was encouraging him to follow pursuit, which would make him happy. Not always agreed with. If he majored in what everyone else wanted, he would never be happy. Living his life on his own terms.

Otherwise, he will be continually searching. Without his friend Hildi he would never find peace. Looking for answers is what brought him to the motorcycle club. Brothers and family are what he truly wanted. It worked for a while until his morals were tested, hence the prison sentence.

A general set of arms reached around Fluffy, turning around to see Miss Lilly as she looked at his face, shaking her head. "We will fix you all up again," hugging Lilly hard, a whisper of, "I missed you," escape from his fresh lips. Breaking the tension, she pointed to her standing on his shoulders.

Lilly spoke, "I never worried when I stood on your shoulders, you would never drop anyone. The strength of you always showed with the grapes of humility." Harold, Snapped, "We grow them good here, don't we?" "Yes, we do." Smiled Lilly. "Time for you boys to head home. I started a fire for you. We'll talk in the morning. Night, boys." Lilly hugs brought with it a comfort. *I'm really home.* As Harold pulled into the carport, Fluffy stood outside, looking at the old homestead, it had been added to over the years, but still a hauntingly large house.

Almost creepy, as if shadows danced until the lights came on. Still, will he ever feel safe again? "Are you gonna stand out there and freeze?" asked Harold. "Ohh sorry. Lost in thought again. Walking into a place that almost had a ghostly feel." Smiling, "Millie left us milk and ginger snaps just like mom used to. Ready to try out a soft bed?" "Yes, but first a long shower." "I get it brother I'll just show you where we keep the soap that doesn't have a rope attached to it."

Fluffy laughs spitting milk through his nose. "Wow you made a joke." 'Ha ha, Reg get your stank button in that shower. I put out a pair of silk pajamas and a robe. See you in the morning." Turning on the hot water, he stood in the shower for what seemed like hours. The pulsating shower head was so nice. Looking at its face in the mirror. Reggie found himself staring at a mirror. "Christ, I look horrible.

No wonder Lilly cried when she saw me," turning out the light.

Reggie slid under the sheets was a down comforter pulled up to his chin. Eyes darting to every corner of the room, safety first.

Once he started to relax his eyes started to flutter. Finally, sleep came. Even though the sun was out, with a couple of inches of sparkling new snow adorning porches. Milly left Reggie's curtains closed. Thinking, *That the boy must be exhausted*. Startled by Millie's presence Reggie, apologized, "Sorry, I'm not used to having someone that close."

Smiling, Millie said, "Breakfast is ready." Putting on a robe, he gently walked down the stairs. The smells coming from the kitchen and we're inviting. Sitting at the dining room table, Reggie felt like royalty. The large cup of coffee was placed in front of him, smiling, he stirred. And it doesn't look like mud. That's a major improvement. Eggs, bacon, toast and orange juice. Reggie looked at Milly and asked,

"What about Harold? Special diet?" "We'll see what Doc Halloway has to say. I would imagine, you will be needing some supplements for your help." Fluffy nodded as he chowed down. "They didn't cook real food, we got slop like you would feed dogs."

Harold announced himself with, "Boy Doc has already called, you get the works." "Well, I would expect nothing less." "Once we get you settled in, we should talk about things." knowing Harold, Reggie says, "Please don't go see the club president on your own."

"Don't worry I will have him brought to my chambers, but I need to find out who's in charge now. The young lady you saved is in witness protection along with her daughter, so they're in no danger. Interesting fact, the club you belong to folded into another branch of the club. Seems many left to join different clubs. What was promised wasn't delivered."

Harold just said, "I had been planning for this since I was notified you were up for release." Looking to his brother, he asked, "You could have been on parole earlier, why the wait?" Thinking a moment, he explained, "I wanted to be free and clear, no parole, no one to answer to and command of my own life, so to speak. I earned my sentence. I took a life, even though it was to protect others. So, I did all my time."

"I understand," Whispered Herald. "Eat up. You have a date with Doc Halloway and Nurse Kelly." "Is she still single?" Snickered Fluffy. Harold snapped, "Let's make sure you're healthy first, shall we?" "Always thinking," smiled Fluffy. "I better get dressed."

Millie looked at Harold. "He is awful pale. A lack of vitamin D&C, what you get from the sun." making scrunched up face. "Sir, he has burned scars and it worries me." Patting Millie's shoulder, "That's why the doctor will give him a complete physical." "I'm guessing he will have different nutritional needs so that might mean more groceries."

"Millie, just let me know what he will need." "Sir, Fruit and real vegetables to start with, and lots of protein. Plus, he will need clothes. He has lost quite a bit of weight." Reggie, laughing loudly, as he rejoins them, "Already planning on fattening me up!?" "OH no, Sir! Just make you healthy, Sir." Giving Millie a gentle squeeze, he knew she truly meant what she said. Harold yelled, "Catch!" A coat was thrown in his direction.

"We will be back later, Millie." Millie shivered as thoughts of his trial came flooding back, and the armed patrols for several weeks after being sentenced. Townspeople who never locked their doors, now we're adding locks and purchasing guns for protection. It was a bad time for their town, but they survived.

No, she knew of the need for the key club, but the town has been through so much. Guess increased population is necessary for the town. Millie has heard talking count about *mixing*. She found it troubling, most of Millie's family had been here from the start of this town. Harold's great grandfather, who was also a judge, passed town ordinance that there was no slave position.

Everyone gets paid for no indentured servitude here. Everyone is free to work in their own town. He had been a leader in progressive treatment of workers for as long as Millie could remember. There had always been a Herald in office, state, county and town. They never really campaigned.

Their reputation for honor and integrity kept them as a fixture in the legal arena. Millie shook her head. She had been lost in thought. “OH, I'd better get back to work.”

Pulling into the parking lot, Harold walked his brother to the office. Nurse Kelly greeted them with a big smile. Laughing, Harold looks at his brother saying, “I will leave him in your capable hands, Nurse Kelly.” Reggie nods, “Sounds good brother.” Then Nurse Kelly informed him. “Let's take some blood.”

That took the wind right out of his sails. After blood and urine analysis, they started with an EKG to make sure that big heart of his still worked.Doc Halloway then entered for the main part of this fiscal after completion. Dale Halloway shook his head in disgust. Harold asks, "So, doc, what's The verdict?" "Well, he is over 20 lbs underweight. He had broken bones that weren't set which will cause issues. He had scars from both physical abuse and cigarette burns; these look like chemical burns. It could be months to a year to get him healthy."

"So, we will start him on iron and vitamins plus a protein rich diet and exercises to help him start the healing process." Dale looks at Reggie, "I would like you to see a psychologist. you has PTSD," Halloway explained. "If you go to touch him, he flinches and retreats. "

"Harold, we have a lot of work to do ahead. I believe that he is afraid of retaliation against our town. But I have filed briefs on the maltreatment of inmates since the warden believes he has the right to sanction torture with his scars. He has no business running a prison."

"It's time he is removed from his lofty perch." "Supreme Court, I am guessing." "Yes, I will need your report, and my brother, along with what he witnessed." Nodding in agreement, Dale knew that this would not go easy. Harold will get justice for those inmates. "So can I go home?" "Sure, I want you to have a visit with this gentleman, a shrink, before you get upset. I noticed some PTSD." Scowling Reggie says, "Well hell yeah, they treated us worse than pigs."

"Do you realize that you flinch and step back when somebody approaches you? When you are approached by me, you flinch."

"No, not really. It's a protection thing, fight or flight." Thinking a moment, he realized it is likely. But being a smarty pants Reggie says, "Nurse Kelly touched me and no Flinting." "That's because you have nothing to fear from her. Physically she's not intimidating for you, but a 250 psycho in a small closed in area is different." "OK Doc, I get it, I will try it" "Maybe sometime in the gym working on those on the heavy bag will help with your displaced frustration."

Reggie laughed. "In other words, take my anger out on the heavy bag." "See," Smile Nurse Kelly, "Not so bad. You can trust us, OK?" "I will, now how about having steak on the penal system's $200 bucks! I'm on my way out the door." Laughed Reggie. Nurse Kelly giggles, "I believe there is some clothes shopping in order." Laughing hard, Reggie snapped. "Kelly, you just wanna see me naked?"

"Ohh I sure do!" laughed nurse Kelly. "Here Kelly, take care our boy out shopping. He needs everything because

I'm not sharing underwear." "Like when we were kids," laughing again Reggie squeals, "you can't fill out my boxers as well as I do." Doc Halloway just shook his head. "Geez, just like high school again, boys. Same routine and all." Handing Kelly cards, Harold said. "Better get going before Doc decides you need to organize something."

Rubbing Reggie's hand, Kelly pulled him through the outer waiting room. As Kelly pulled out of the parking lot, Harold said. "Now what else did you find?" "I think he might have had a seizure or a stroke during his incarceration. There are some areas on his head CT from the Infirmary that are troubling. Blows to the head can cause these lesions.

Other things like being thrown down a flight of stairs. There are many causes. The doctor from the Infirmary will hand off records I need."

"I had asked about the autopsy prep. I think that the warden could be selling body parts. I believe our boy Fluffy has seen things he shouldn't have seen. So, head trauma was their reminder to ***keep your mouth shut***." "Well, remembered your blood pressure you have every right to be angry, but you need to keep a clear head if you intend to stop this barbarous behavior. Warden Seaman seems to feel convicts are throw away people, no one will miss them."

"So how does this play out?" "Their doctor will feed us proof, but only if he can practice elsewhere." "In other words, he wants to work with us." Harold said, "I would need to see what he brings to the table." Standing quietly Lilly listened as they spoke of the horror happening in the convicts, Harold realized someone was behind him. "So, you heard?" "Yes, I did. And frankly, if you can't bring down that

SOB warden, I have plenty of contacts in the governor's office, among others."

Looking at Reggie's chart a gasp let loose from her perfectly painted lips. "My God they worked *our boy* over constantly." "Seems he was their pet project to torture devices, and he never complained because he thought he deserved it for taking the light." "Poor baby," whispered Lilly. Harold just said, "He needs to get better before I explain the Key Club." Lilly softly spoke, "I would agree Harold, he needs to concentrate on feeling better. So, did he sleep?"

"Yes, but before he could allow himself to. He checked all the corners, with a whisper of safety first." "Poor boy was afraid he would be attacked in his sleep. Such a shame." "Well, I am heading to my offices to see how well received my filings against the maltreatment went." Lilly headed back to her shop.

While Doc called to plan to meet his new Allie. Duwanna greeted Harold at the doors with two fistfuls of phone messages. As he sorted through them, "These are about putting off their divorce hearings. There were two with no return phone numbers and four from Superior Court."

"The Attorney General's message was concise. We need a meeting. Warden Zieman is already under investigation." "Looks like a busy day, Joanna. I will be having lunch here in my office, and I don't want to be disturbed." "I will head out to get your lunch order." "Before you leave, I will need the minutes of the town board meeting from last night." "They are on your desk, in a green folder Sir. May I ask how your brother is?" "He's OK, adjusting to better accommodations and showering alone." "Oh dear, I am heading out. Sir, I checked on Roz, she looks better, not so green." "That's good." Smiled Harold.

"Judith still a question mark. Lisa is pleased as punch and feels just fine." Looking at the messages with no return number, *seems suspicious*. Calling the AGA, Judge Harold calling, a voice on the other end says, "Hi Harold." "So, what's going on Hank?" "Seems our creepy warden has been using inmates to furnish body parts needed for transplants and he makes a tidy profit." "As the AGA I will need the proof that you are basing this on."

"Doc Halloway saw things that threw up red flags. Example: a dock at the Infirmary was setting up for what looked like an autopsy.

He is also willing to give Dale the files, but the fact that the warden sanctions torture by the guards is a serious problem. First, because their inmates don't mean they have no rights. He used his position as a warden to be judge and jury. I sent you a copy of my brother's physical, along with what has been seen last night." Hank then asked, "What is your ultimate goal here Judge Harold?"

"To remove Warden Seaman, along with those guards, and to clean it up. Reggie didn't fight the brutality because he believed he earned his eight years for accidentally taking the life, but he endured some horrible torture at their hands, and I am sure they treat all inmates according to their form of justice."

"So where is our favorite football star?" "Nurse Kelly took him shopping. He's 20 lbs underweight, so he needs to refresh his wardrobe. Kelly will watch for any signs of trouble, cognitive." "I took a peek. Seizures or a stroke, and head trauma. I guess they wanted him sedate and quiet. I checked in with the Marshalls and they are doing fine. No one has approached her or her daughter. I made sure that they were aware that Reggie was out so club members may come out. I would like to order protection at your place."

Harold shaking his head explains, "That would be like a neon sign. Hey, I'm over here. Plus, I have a pretty big arsenal at the house. But I did receive 2 phone calls with no call back numbers," Hank says, "How about a trap and trace for your office phone?" "Against my better judgment, yes, I guess so."

"I will let you know when it's ready. Harold, what's the chances of the club coming to your town?" "Truthfully, I am not sure. I have heard the clubs split off joining other charters or other clubs. If I had to guess they will arrive after things are more relaxed, not on guard." "So how goes your other project?" "What are you asking about?" "Look, everyone in four counties knows about Key Club."

"They're confirmed pregnancies so no problems." "No, Reverend Thomas, the Auxiliary bitching periodically, but not much else, just a bit of jealousy because they weren't invited." "Other towns are looking at your town as the mothership of sorts to lead the other towns." A knocking at Harold's door. "I better let you go. My lunch has arrived."

Duwanna entered with his lunch, "Were on the phone a while because I have been waiting out there for you to finish." "The AGA was who I was speaking with." "Oh, I see, so I will let you eat in peace." "Have you seen my brother?" "Last I saw he was being dragged off into

Miss Lilly's Salon for the full treatment." Snickering Harold says, "Well, I am sure he is enjoying the attention." "Oh, I bet, the cold shopping would have been amusing to watch.

Kelly asked me to return your credit cards with receipt so you can keep track of the expenditure. Oh, and Lilly's full treatment is on the House. Something about a protein patch for his scalp." Laughing, Harold knew he was in good hands. "Her shaves are so good your face feels as soft as a baby's bottom, but her straight razor is sharp, so keeping her happy is a must."

Halfway through the afternoon green tea, Fluffy came bouncing through the door like a playful baby lion. "Boy, you seem chipper Bud," smiled Harold. "Had a great day. I loved all those ladies fussing all over me and enjoyed every minute of it. So, steak dinner tonight," smiled Fluffy.

The look on Herald face gave way to concern. “Who is mad now?”

He showed his brother the phone messages with no callback numbers. “It wouldn't help. They never kept the same 1 so that's why you are getting a trap and trace."" How did you know Reggie? The phone guy looks familiar from your apartment?” Asked Harold. “Yeah, I am sure. Well, I invited Miss Lilly to come with us.” Thinking for a minute, he called his favorite steakhouse. Speaking with the manager, “He will have the private dining room ready for us.”

“So, guess you can spend that 200.” “Well, some, but less than 200 because I saw your favorite cigars and wanted to say thank you for being my Big Brother.” “Now you like me,” chuckled Harold. “At least I haven't tied you to the tackle, dummy. You were an asshole, but you were always shoulder to shoulder with me at the first sign of trouble." "Fluffy, remember us against six guys?" "Yeah, but they're never getting back to our town football game again. We were a pretty good team in a fight."

"OK, let me get cleaned up before we pick up Lilly." "Kelly already gave Millie my new clothes, so 7.1 with Nurse Kelly. Yeah, she was willing to let me blubber on about my colorful history in prison. Plus, she arranged for me to see mental health about PTSD."

"Those are good reasons to talk with a professional. So, I talked to the AGA and they already have an investigation rolling. He had a copy of my filings in hand. So, Dale's new friend will provide us with proof of abuse and its own body part. No more Warden Seamen if I had my way," Harold announced.

"Plus, this bird, they were all in on it. Anyone seem interested in you while you were out with Kelly?" "No. No one even looked in my direction." "That's the way we want it. Let's get a move on. Lilly will be waiting." Standing in the doorway, giggling was Lilly. "You boys gossip, like a bunch of women." "Do we have time to clean up?" "Harold, you look fine, I told Millie we were going out for dinner." Walking towards the outer office, Herald yelled, "Don't forget to lock up Duwanna." "Yes Sir, I will."

Heading out, Harold noticed a car in the parking lot. Not from their town. Looking towards the driver's seat, walking to the car, Harold realized he knew him. "I know you," growled Harold. "Yes Sir, you do." Showing his prison badge, Reggie knew immediately. "Hey Doc," "My proper name is Ferguson, or Gus for short. I am here to meet Doctor

Halloway." Nodding towards the office, "You will find him in his office" Dale came jogging over. "Hey Gus, Harold, Reggie, Miss Lilly of course." A quick phone call and Harold added more people to the private dining room, motioning to them.

"Let's head out to the steakhouse." Once they arrived an order of sweet tea all around sent the waitress scampering off. "An order of stake, fries and salad all around, plus some to start with." Pulling out files out of his briefcase, Gus looked at Lilly, questioning how much she knows fluffy.

"You know that hot cheerleader from our football games? This is our prom queen." Gus spoke quietly, "Damn I wish I had played football now too. Let me guess, Honor Society? "Math achievements, OK, so I am old school," handing Dale the files, Doc Halloway gasped at the torture the inmates endured, all for money." "Exactly, Warden Seaman believes, Inmate lives don't count."

"That is sad as a point of view. Prison is supposed to be a point of rehabilitation, not selling body parts like car parts!" "Unfortunately, that's not all. Staged fights to keep troublemakers in mind. If it's a head injury, the rest of the meat is still good, just like a deer." Doc Halloway was so angry that they perverted the Hippocratic Oath. "I will need to make copies of all of these so you can put them back, Justin."

Their dinners arrived, which lit up the mood at the table. The boys told stories from back in the day. Gus noticed how welcoming they were. As they were closing the restaurant, Harold slipped away, files in hand, knowing the owner gave him access to the office equipment. Harold looked a bit confused about the food orders that covered the machine. The waitress walked by looking into her boss's office. She knew Harold would need assistance.

She removed the stack of orders, filled the paper tray, and showed Harold the tricks to using this old copy machine. After what seemed like an eternity, the copies were completed. Returning to the table, Harold handed the file back to Gus, "Put it back, and make sure everything goes back to normal." Nodding, Gus affirms, "Yes Sir." "I will give the AGA the OK to clear you for your help."

"Watch your back Judge. That warden has eyes throughout the tri-county area." Leaving ahead of his new friends, Gus felt secure in the fact that Judge Harold was one of the good guys.

However, Lilly had concerns of her own. "If our town gets flooded by feds, what about our Key Club?" The drive home was eerily quiet but uneventful, dropping Lilly off. The boys got a kiss on the cheek and a good night.

The ride home was strangely quiet. Reggie spoke. "You just tired Herald?" "Some," he said nodding. He patted his brother. "I know Harold." As Harold flipped on the lights. "What do you think you know, brother?" "Well, I hear talk about a swingers club to help repopulate our town." "And what else have you heard?"

"That if we don't bring our census up, we could have to fold into another counter county." "This project is kind of like a mothership. If it goes well then, the other towns will follow suit. Since you already know, I guess I don't have to explain, do I?"

Nodding, Reggie spoke up. "I know these decisions have been hard on you." "The pressure is enormous." "So, have you talked with Hildi about it? I know you still talk with her daily. Give her my regards. I miss her. I am heading to bed, freedom is tiring."

Harold laughed a bit. "Never thought of freedom as tiring," but then again, he has never had his freedom taken away. *Living in an oversized pen can and must have been tough*.

Heading to his study, he poured himself a Brandy, lit a cigar and sat down. "Hello Hildi, I wanted you to know our boy Reggie is home now. It will take us a while to get him settled in."

Thumbing through the file from Gus, Harold shuddered. "Ohh, Hildi, they mistreat those boys in that place, tortured for amusement of that bastard Warden Seaman!" His eyes watered with anger. "Hildi, how do we fix this? The law can only do so much, but he deserves much more than the law allows. Our boy has been put through so much, all for doing the right thing." Pulling himself together, he says, "We have 3 confirmed pregnancies, so the plan is starting to bear fruit. I miss you so much. Reggie also sends his regards. He misses you too. Goodnight my love. I will see you soon but not yet. There's work to be done first."

Speaking to Hildi always helps him center his heart and brain to work together. "Goodnight, my love." Putting out his cigar, he finished his branding and headed off to bed. An extremely cold chill enveloped his body, pushing through his to his soul. *Evil is coming, but when?*

Feeling ill at ease, Harold checked doors and windows, making sure all was secure. Just then a smack of a window disturbs his thoughts. He went looking until he found the open shutter smacking against the house. Reaching for the window, Harold pulled in and fastened the latch. *Note to self, have Carpenter fix the shutter.*

Heading back upstairs once more, he readied himself for bed. Pulling his covers up to his chin, Harold's eyes danced. Between darkened corners of his chambers, until sleep finally pulled him under for dreams.

He truly didn't want his father pointing at him accusingly. "Why do you get the right to play God?" with a small boy voice "But Father, we will lose our town without the Key Club." "So, you just wanna play God? Isn't that why you became a judge?" "Power over life and death of our town and its residents is what we do father."

Then his mother came into focus. "Our Lord wants no one before him. You are putting yourself. Above God and his Holy Word, it will never be allowed. God will smite thee!"

Harold's eyes snapped open, wide awake. He knew he was up for a while. His parents in a dream usually meant Harold was conflicted about his decisions. *The Key Club, but truthfully, was the only option to benefit the town. Other towns are trying options along these lines as well. Maybe some warm milk will help me get back to sleep.* To his surprise, Reggie had the same idea. "Mom and Dad interrupt your sleep too." "I am afraid so, brother. Usually, I get how disappointed in me they are." Harold laughed. "Yeah, they feel I'm playing God, and I have no right in doing so. I get yelled at now more than when we were kids." Pouring the warm milk, Reggie sat down, while Harold appeared a secret stash of cookies.

"Nice score brother." "We did this all the time as kids right for a game." "Yep, Mom always kept the cookie stashed away. I bet she did that on purpose so Dad didn't know. Like finding money rolled into your socks." Smiling, Reggie cackled. "Mom understood until you failed English, and then she became your personal tutor." "But, it was better than dad in history or math. I still have the knots on my head from where Dad smacked me for the wrong answer." "Yeah, I guess our parents had plans for us."

"I believe all parents have expectations on what their prodigy will be. So which kind of cookies, fudge royal or peanut butter?" Asked Harold. Laughing loudly Reggie replied, "Both. No parents to bitch at us for being pigs." After enjoying cookies and milk, they returned to their rooms for some sleep.

Quietly, Millie entered the house to start the morning prep, only to find a note. ***Sleeping in this morning. No calls please.*** Looking around the kitchen, Millie discovered the evidence of a cookie eating event, laughing softly. She understood. Scampering around planning her dinner for the evening meal took time, but new recipes will help. She would have to incorporate 2 diet plans for each meal. Millie had plans to speak with Nurse Kelly on options for their diets. Ironing and hanging Reggie's new clothes will be a new chore.

At around 8:00 AM, Reggie came bounding into the kitchen, "How is Miss Millie this morning?" "Fine, Sir, and yourself? Are you good, Sir?" "Oh, these are mine. I will take them up for you Millie." "But can I ask you why you washed my brand-new clothes?" Because Sir, other people touch anything and they try them on. At least if I wash them first, I know they are clean." "Sounds reasonable to me, Millie."

Harold spoke, "Remember Mom did that too. Women are like that, clean is important. Remember tug of War and the mud pit?" crack Herald. Reggie cackled, "Yep, us two against 6 guys." Millie said. "Who won?"

"We did but covered in mud. Mom hosed us off outside first with cold water before we were allowed to come in the house." Millie started giggling. "Sir, you mean like this?" In her hand was a picture of Harold & Reggie covered from head to toe and mud at the fair, holding a trophy above their head. "Damn, why so much mud?" Reggie cracks, "With shit! I couldn't get the mud out of my ears for a week." "Breakfast is ready, gentlemen. Coffee is already on the table. I went western Turkey bacon, orange juice and toast lightly buttered. I followed both diets to make sure you boys stay healthy."

"So, what's for dinner tonight?" "Vegetarian lasagna. Lunch is vegetable beef soup, fruit cup with a tuna melt." Reggie smiled, "I would like to go over to the bowling alley to see Frank and Rose." Harold nods, "Just stay with them and we will slowly reintroduce you to the town."

"OK brother, I trust you know best." Dressing in jeans, thermal underwear, shirt with a flannel, and hunting jacket. Harold asked, "Reggie, would you come to the garage?" Pulling back a cover, there was an old Galaxy painted a deep red with Chrome. Fluffy had tears welling up." I thought she had gone to the scrap yard." "No, I figured you would need some wheels. I had her refreshed and road ready. Insured, so here you go." Passing him the keys. "Now to find you a job after you heal up. Lord knows with that face you could stare a starving dog off a meat wagon." "Nice brother, nice."

Starting up the car, Fluffy was filled with memories of teenage, filled hormones. No girl could say no to a ride in his car. Pulling up to the bowling alley. Knocking on the back door, and he heard Frank yell, "Deliveries are at the other door!"

Opening the door, Reggie cracked. "Putting me to work already Frank?" The voice did not sound familiar to Frank. Coming around the corner, Frank dropped the box of sausage. "Holy shit, Fluffy, is that really you!?! Oh my Lord!" With hugs and backslaps he was greeted warmly. Roz came around the corner still a bit green toned, but feeling a bit better. "Hi." Rosalyn's ice cream came from her lips. “My Lord, Reggie?” “Yes, Roz, it's me.” “OH, my boy, look at you!” “It looks worse than it feels. So how does business go?” “We are hanging in there.” Frank casually asked, “So the sentence is complete?”

“Yes and no parole.” “What are you driving?” “Remember the old Galaxy? She's outside.” “Christ, we ran that poor car into the dirt.” “Remember the wreck? And how we pulled the dents out in auto body class?” “It took three months before your parents found out.” “They were angry until they found out we fixed it in the auto body class, and he didn't have to pay, so he was OK about the crash.” Smiling at Roz, he handed her a stack of photographs.

Looking through each picture brought back fond memories. Roz was a varsity cheerleader and her long dark hair cascading down her back with a satin ribbon adorning her ponytail.

Before they could start to reminisce, Judith arrived for coffee. Sneaking up behind her, Fluffy grabbed her around the waist, twirling her around. Judith, flailing helplessly at Fluffy. He just laughed, spun her around so she was nose to nose with him. “Is it really you, Reggie?” “I think so. I'm wearing his underwear.”

Laughing hard, Judith hugged him. “OH, it really is you!” “Yes, I am here.” “So how is living with your brother the judge?” “Is it just like where we picked up and left off.” “So, I thought I would visit for a while, if that's alright. You know my brother, he would never miss a day of work.” Helping Frank put freight away. Frank made Fluffy feel useful.” So, the girls are pregnant, and thus the women are a bit grouchy."

Little Rose Marie came in with, "Daddy, did you get momma's medicine?" Ambling over to the counter, he handed her a brown bag stapled shut, "With two kisses for the messenger." Looking at Fluffy, she asked, "Do I know you?" "Yes, here's a picture of me holding you. I was on the Rescue Squad and I helped deliver you." Rose Marie thought for a minute then said, "My momma says you wrapped me up and carried me like a football." Laughing a bit, Fluffy said, "I guess I did." "Well, we like you, so you can stay here in our town."

"Why thank you, Rose Marie." "At least you are remembered fondly." Frank smiled. Kal came in with, "Dad. Mom. I forgot about my field trip. It must be signed now, or I can't ride the bus." Filling it out fast, he handed it back. Smirking,

Kal grabbed the old football and yelled, “Catch!” Fluffy went long to catch a perfect spiral.

“Welcome home dude. I will beat you on the lanes later Reggie.” “Frank. Your boys will do great in college.” “True, but I will guarantee they picked the furthest school away from us. It's all a part of the growing process.” “So, who's hiring around here?” “Post office and food delivery. So, nothing further furthering your education inside?”

“No, just learning how to survive in that hole.” “Christ, how long you've been out?” “Little over 48 hours. Nurse Kelly took me clothes shopping. Good ol’ Doc Halloway gave me a full on physical to make sure I am healthy.” “So how about we have you come over for dinner?” “Sure, Doc says I'm 20 lbs under what he feels I should be, so your wife's cooking should help with that. Harold seems a bit busy today, well when he gets a burr in his butt he just doesn't quit." "Seems the AGA flagged brothers filing." "Why?" "Seems they were already investigating the prison and Warden Seamen. Can't step on each other's toes, don't you know?"

"Yeah, lawyers are an anal bunch." "So, I was told to ease myself back in with the town folks." "Ah, checking the temperature of the town." "Yes, he was figuring you might get a cool reception." Frank said, "Not by anyone who knew you, except maybe Reverend Thomas and his judgmental auxiliary ladies." Laughing loudly Fluffy said, "Not so judgmental when it came to drinking, smoking or shrinking. We have pictures." "OH, that would be great for Miss Lilly's picture board."

Telling Frank was enjoying those memories, but he knew he'd better get back to work. "It's a league night." "I'd better get back. Millie has my lunch planned." "Stop in later for some practice." "Seems your son is eager to play." "He has been so good helping with the house and the kids since Moms Under the Weather." Reggie questioned, "The kids have no idea what the Key Club is, do they?" "Not yet, the adults still aren't sure about its outcome. Anyone bother you from your old club?" "Nope, not yet."

"Keep low profile for some time, but if you want some work to help build muscle I can offer you unloading trucks." "Sure, I could use a good workout, Frank." "We will see you later for the league?" "Sure Frank, not a problem." Heading home, he thought about how stifled the townspeople became, looking towards the church where Reverend Thomas watched his flock from a lofty perch.

Passing judgment on the followers. Before Fluffy went home, he decided to speak with Reverend Thomas. The drive Over was short with people staring as he drove by, marching up the stairs. With purpose in his heart as he opened the door to the red carpet and stained glass were almost cold, distant feeling. Thomas said, "May I help you?"

Walking toward the Reverend he felt a slap of cold air as he approached Thomas. The closer he got, the more confused Thomas seemed. Thomas stared down the stairs with a steel gaze, like he was about to take on the devil himself. Reverend Thomas asked, "Do I know of you?" "You should. You presided over my baptism as your father took ill." "Still having trouble placing you son." Harold spoke from the back of the Chapel. "Of course you know him." After a few minutes Reverend Thomas spoke, "Reginald Beauford Harold."

"It's been a minute since I have heard my full name used with such disdain, Sir." "Weren't you sent to prison?" "Yes Sir, I was." "So, are you here to ask for absolution?" "No Sir, but I want to let you know I was back home." "You have *no* need for absolution?"

"Reverend Thomas, I killed the man accidentally, but it was in protection of a woman and her daughter. So no, I paid the price. I did my time. Because of this, those women are safe from repercussions of my behavior." "I heard they were put in protective custody." Thomas explained, "Even though your crime was done in protection of others, I cannot condone it." Before Harold could speak, Reggie spoke.

"I was taught everyone was welcome to church fellowship. So, are you telling me that my parents taught me wrong?" "No, your parents were correct, son. But small towns never forget or forgive." "I thought it was your job to help your congregation to continue spreading God's love and forgiveness, for when he returns to bring home his flock. I would hate to be in this crowd. It's a shame, Reverend." Reverend Thomas interjects, "I never said you weren't invited to join us." "Ah, but actions speak louder than words, every time."

Harold just shook his head. "Pompas is polite," growled Fluffy. "Man, I never thought our town would allow such BS. Let's go. Millie has lunch ready." While sitting at the dining room table, Reggie got really upset. "I knew I shouldn't have come back home." Harold frowned, "You belong here as much as anyone else in this town." "Why are they so damn hateful? Even in prison you were given a small dance. I bet you caught all kinds of crap over the Key Club." Harold said, "Yes, but some of it was jealousy because they weren't invited to join. As Miss Lilly would say, some of the most pristine causes have the biggest skeletons in them, and she knows all of them."

"Glad she's on our side. Hey brother?" Nodding as he shoveled in his tuna melt. "I wouldn't want to piss her off. Senators and congressmen ask her for her opinion and advice." "So what's your next event?" "Valentine's Day event, but it's just for married couples." "I see" "When you Arrive keys go in in a bowl, and then facing forward a lady puts her hand in, grabs the key and they are paired up. Hopefully there will be babies from the events. Just trying to save our town from going under." "It's a good idea, but kids will ask questions. It won't take them long to figure it out. So how do you raise these new children?"

"As a community, just as we've always done. Believe it or not, Reggie, less divorces and separations because now they have another way to deal with needs. Well, it has already made things better at home. Trying harder, I believe. Almost a competition in performance." Reggie cackled. "And no man likes to be outdone by another." "Women are putting more work into their appearance." "So how do I get an invite?"

"It's just for married folks, you can't show up to the event without your spouse. That way it keeps a fair playing field. There's no bragging either, but many of the men are performing better at their jobs also," explained Harold. Reggie asked, "Rules?" "Yes, just to keep everyone honest. No feelings hurt. If a problem arises, it's brought to me, and the ladies go to Lilly."

"Who's in charge of the kids while parents are out" "The kids usually have a party at the bowling alley." "Well, I could help out with entertaining the kids." "OK, I'm sure you'd be more fun than Reverend Thomas." "Always," laughed Fluffy.

"Even little kids like me." "That's because little kids climb all over you like a jungle gym," cracked Harold. "Now I have to go back to work, but Miss Lilly could use your help. Decorations need to be carried." "No problem. Tell her I will head to her shop, but Kal and I are going to throw a few balls at the bowling alley." "Bet the coach could use help with the rifle team. Some of the boys are pissy, cause girls could try out."

"Ohh some bruised egos," laughed fluffy. "Exactly. So, it's not a smooth combination. They need to figure out women are just as capable as men." "Hell, I was a crack shot, but then dad demanded perfection in all we did." "Well, you know, he was hard on us because he felt we had great potential." Smiled Herald. "Bet that isn't how he feels now," looking up toward the heavens. "He'd have been proud of you for protecting those ladies. And you were honest and you did the time. That's where his raising us came in."

"Your compassion and love for the towns people came from Mom. Your heart is full of love and big is a mountain my brother." "Thanks Harold." "I guess they underestimated you, brother." "Yeah, just because I am a large man doesn't mean I am an abusive man. I want people to understand I am fluffy like cotton."

"If they saw you play football they might not agree," laughing, "but it was all in good fun." "Said a one-man defensive line." "You better get going. You know how Miss Lilly is and feels about late arrivals." Grabbing his keys he headed to Lilly's "Miss Lilly, are you here?" called Fluffy. "Yes, she's out back with deliveries and decorations for the Valentine's Day event."

Coming up behind Lilly, Reggie grabbed her waist with a swift turn, Lilly swung. Fluffy caught her hand long before she could hit his face. "Too slow Lilly," smiled Reggie. "Fluffy, I man can get hurt sneaking up on a lady." "Sorry Lilly, just having fun." "Come on, let's put those arms to use." "Lead the way Lilly."

Arriving at the Beaver, she acknowledged, "We have our events here. It's out of town without prying eyes." As the decorations were being hung, Lilly looked at him. "I will assume Harold explained our dire straits." Pulling out from a large leather tote bag, "If you look at our census, we need more births and even strangers at this point otherwise our town will fail."

"Noone realized it was this bad?" Questioned Reggie. "Not until Harold got the census report. Unfortunately, our town is not the only one. Our whole county is in dire straits. The trustees are already cutting funding to towns that have a low census count."

"Gods' honest truth. We would even accept your biker friends. We need warm bodies so to speak. Christ, even the Amish or anyone else would start a place here." "What about the teens? They will eventually figure it out." "That is a possibility, but hopefully we will have the answers for them." "So basically, it's a sociological experiment." "Kind of," smiles Lilly.

"Damn it and I thought the social levels in prison were difficult. This has it beat!" "Let me fill in the blanks. More divorces, more separations, no sex between married folks. Plus, soldiers that have come home aren't ok." Lilly smiled, "You understand." "But how does all this work?" "Children will be raised by the Community, so there's no ostracizing the children."

"This seems almost logical except for the auxiliary ladies." "Yes, they are a problem. We try to keep the club members out of church if at all possible." "Really, wouldn't that be like advertising it?" "Never said they were the brightest. Just ignorant." "Well, the welcome I got from Reverend Thomas lacked A brotherly tone. Apparently, I have not atoned for my sins properly."

"Oh, my friend, there are closets that have many, many skeletons." "So, of course, they can stand on all the bones to look down on." cracked Reggie, "I see you have encountered their wrath." "Not exactly Lilly, but I told him how I felt about the hypocrisy from the church. I need to get this done, I promised Kal a few games at the bowling alley. Harold wants me to go slow, to immerse myself back in town business."

"Harold is ashamed of you!?!" Growled Lilly. "No, but he knows people associate prison with a horrible person, even though it happened in protection of others. I committed a mortal sin. I accidentally took a life. People here don't forgive or forget." "That is such bullshit. Plus, I am proud of you as a man, as a friend, so I better never hear you put yourself down or doubting your moral compass. Your heart is as big as a mountain. Very rare quality fluff."

A hug quieted his hurt and anger about the townspeople. Because of the people's double standards, it makes him question coming home. But he also knew why he needed home, even though Harold wouldn't admit to it. His steadfast brother needed him. Reggie shifted, "I need to get cleaned up." Kal would be waiting.

Wandering in the side door, he could smell Millie's cooking. "Hello Sir, would you like a snack before dinner?" "No, Millie, I'm saving my belly for dinner, but I need a shower." "Sir, Kal called. He said be there at 8:00 PM. He reserved a lane?" Laughing Reggie says, "Roz's son thinks he can beat me!" "Be kind, Sir, he's just a boy." Cackling. "He's man enough to challenge an older man than he can take his ass kicking on the alley."

"What else did you do today, Sir?" "Every time you say Sir, I start looking for my dad. So, call me Fluff, or Reggie. I helped Miss Lilly with decorations." "With your added height I am sure it went faster." Nodding, "I would agree." Reggie ran up the stairs just like back in school. Buttoning his shirt, as he ran back down the stairs. "Oh Sir, I mean Reggie. Several phone calls with very little said. Something about delivering your old bike?" Harold walked in before Fluffy could answer. "Sounds like your old friends." Millie looked too Reggie, "From a Lifetime ago. Are you sure, Sir?"

"Yes, I felt I had nowhere to keep my bike when I was inside." Looking to Harold, Milly asks, "They're bad men, aren't they?" "Nothing for you to worry about." Harold commented offhandedly.

As Millie started to serve the meal, the phone rang. Harold says, "I've got it." Answering from his study, he growled. "Hello." "Yes, we are trying to make a connection with the R.B. We have his motorcycle. I am sure he will need it back." Nodding, "Where can I meet up with you? I will be glad to pay the storage fees." "He's not out?" "He is in a psychiatric facility. The poor boy just broke down. I can have a record pick up his bike?" "Let me ask my pop."

Harold had a wrinkled brow. *Why would a club put a kid up to calling? I smell a club rat.* "Can you meet my dad at the Depot Inn? At 8:30 PM." "Sure, that will be fine." Listening, Reggie was afraid for his brother. Joining Millie and Reggie, he began to eat. Knowing this would be a private conversation. Reggie growled, "What the fuck do you think you're doing?" "Meeting the man that says he has your bike." "A psych center Herald!?!" "It caught them off guard, and I have already made arrangements with a towing company. Plus, the mechanics are undercover officers. I will be prepared for all outcomes."

"Geez it could be a disaster. You realize they are going to want paperwork proving I was admitted!" "The AGA helped Doc Halloway with the paperwork to make it look legit. So continue with your trip to the bowling alley." "But Harold." "No buts I will handle this. Stay here in town. Millie will drop you off, no one will expect it. I will pick you up at closing. I want to check on Roz anyway."

As Reggie got ready, Millie started the dishwasher. "Let's go Reggie, I want to tuck my babies in for bed." "House keys and wallet, check." Heading out Millie gave all clear nod. Pulling out a shotgun, with rounds, just as a peacekeeping idea. Using a kid to call was dirty pool, knowing Reggie would come out of hiding to protect a child.

Pulling in, Harold hit the horn, and outcomes his partner. “The papers are all here. So, what's up?” “Not sure, but they used the kid to call for him. Sneaky, aren't they?” “Well, most clubs dabble in illegal options.” “But he had to ask his dad if the meeting was acceptable. Strange thing for a badass biker.”

“Maybe he was playing around trying to get invited to join. The Depot Inn is out in no man's land, hence mechanics, but truly undercover cops?” “It’s just in case we need a Hail Mary play. I don't have a gun, but I have a baton leftover from martial arts training. In a fight everything is useful.” “I see you believe bigger is better, Harold. Shotguns leave very large holes in whatever they shoot at. See my point?”

"Dale, I'm glad it's you and not your dad. Why people admired him." "As you know, we had words about Hilda's pain and letting her go. I understand the Hippocratic Oath just not how you can't relieve the pain by death. She was in constant pain, no control over her bladder or bowels." "Even though your dad couldn't sanction it. He never needed an autopsy and signed her death certificate as complications from treatment." "I will always be grateful for that."

"Here we are, and if it goes bad, just remember you are my best friend." "Thanks Judge. Such emotion from you." "Shut up asshole." Laughed Harold.

Harold and Dale made sure they had a view of the entrance and exit. If by magic several large clad men in leather descended on their booth. "So, do we have to introduce each other?" "I think we're pretty well known to each other." "Are you sure?" "Well, let me think a moment. Are you, Judge Harold and have messed up our delivery system." "Selling drugs and guns to kids was not acceptable, and selling guns to kids is not cool either. But FYI, most farm kids have been shooting a rifle by the age of five, so most of them come expert marksmen for the military." Nodding, he smiled. "Harold, you can call me president."

"So, prove to me our boy has gone off his rocker." "Technically it is PTSD, like soldiers get after serving," handing off the papers. "President explains we have connections too, so we will know if it's fake." Chatting about an early spring, his man confirming the papers to be legit. "Now what am I ***really*** here for?" "Well, we do know about the Key Club, so. We know you think outside the box if you will."

"Look Reggie did the right thing to protect those ladies. I wasn't old enough to challenge my father's authority. He was wrong. I have been working on our rules, adjusting them. Times have changed. Our club is trying legit businesses, but we are here to return his property. No ill will and he can come back. Most of the men that followed my father had either left to join a different charter or died by the regime they followed. So, I would like to part ways as friends. Also, I will give my private number in case your town needs us."

Not accepting their newfound club rules. "What do you really want, boys?" "I have been in the legal system for over 20 years. So, when's the other shoe gonna drop?" "Well, we would like to know how you established your key club. Our hometown is facing the same demise. So, we contacted your friend Lilly. She said she could put together a basic outline for us. Maybe the Doc, there could talk ours through the preparations for babies." "One hard and fast rule. All participants must have a spouse. If one doesn't want to come to an event, their other half isn't welcome without him or her. That way, no jealousy. The rules are simplistic but effective." as Lilly came in all eyes turned towards her.

"Hello gentlemen." Looking to Herald, he nodded. Before laying out her perfect project, Lilly asked, "Don't you think we should sign our NDR so no one talks about our agreement? I am also a notary, so how about it?" reading the papers, the Prez said, "OK, let's sign this baby." All parties signed with Lily's notary stamp in place. "Now let's get his bike on the back of the wrecker." Lilly smile. "Does it run?" "Yes ma'am. Wanna take it for a spin?" Grabbing the helmet and keys. Once it started, she ran the parking lot like a racehorse. "Miss Lilly, since when are you equipped to ride a motorcycle?" Asked Harold. "I have been married several times. I know my way around the man's engine."

"That is one hell of a woman," commented president. "Damn it, I have an old lady or I would sweep Miss Lilly off her feet." "Young man. Many have tried, but not many can say they succeeded". "If only," Harold broke. "She's more woman than most men can handle." "Amen!" As the boys latched the motorcycle down, the President Pulls out a large box from Reggie's apartment. "This picture is how I knew who you were." "So, now that we are friends. I have questions also. Let's start with Warden Seaman and his guards." "That deal was done before I was old enough to take office." "Do you do you do business with him?" "No, why?"

"FYI, there's an investigation, he's using inmates for selling body parts!" "God dammit, thanks for letting us know. You know how your doc noticed the inmate who is having a seizure or a stroke? He was my cousin, and that saved his life. He was sent to the hospital. So, thanks, Doc. You are good people, considering you are a judge and the others a doctor."

The drive home was deafening. "So, what's on your mind, Dale?" "You warned them about the investigation?" "Yes, it's called goodwill. Not enough information to tank the investigation, but enough to prove we are trustworthy. And I recorded it all so both Reggie and the ADA know what was said." "OK, so you are OK with telling your brother you made a deal?" "Yes, it was a fair deal. So, everyone stays safe."

As each departed in separate areas, Harold went to the bowling alley. Walking in, he can hear Fluffy howling like a kid. "So, who's winning?" "It's a tie." "No rematch because I have homework to do." "Later Dudes!" Smiled Fluffy. Looking at Harold. "So, what's the damage?" "Listen to my recording of our visit and you can judge for yourself." As Reggie listened, he knew the paperwork was bogus, but they bought it. "They returned your property, including the picture used to identify me."

After listening twice, Reggie knew the idea was to keep people from getting hurt because of his history. Arriving home to warm milk and butter cookies filled with jam. "So, Lilly was riding around the parking lot on my bike?" While stuffing his face with cookies. "Yes, even I didn't see that one coming. So, the paperwork is signed and notarized, so no backing out." Retrieving a large box, Harold set it on the table.

"What's left from your apartment Reggie." Looking through the pictures from a life he once had, a sad smile crossed his face looking at Hildi's funeral announcement from the society page. "You understand why I couldn't stay Herald. I loved her too. We shared so much together. I had to go away."

"So, where's my lady?" "She's parked in the garage out of the weather." "Lady Blue still sounds great," touching the handlebars. Outback, floods of memories, how hard it was to get patched and loyal to the club came first and foremost. "Here's a cover for your bike, Reggie. She'll be ready when you are. Let's hit the rack. There will be plenty of gossip in the morning." "So, what were you and Doc going to do with a shotgun and a baton against the club of bikers?" "Not a whole hell of a lot, just put up a show." "Well, it worked, but for how long is another story. I bet doc was scared." "Not as bad as you would have imagined. Lilly showed absolutely No Fear. She referred to them as gentlemen. The new president even wished he was single so he could pursue Lilly."

Laughing hard enough for milk to squirt out his nose. Reggie was shocked! "See handled without violence or blood spatter. "So, what did he want in return for his generosity?" "Seems a town he is fond of his having the same census issues we are having." "Wanted your basic plan to start their own version of their own club?" "Guess all the towns are in the same state and are trying to create more census. I would stay in town just in case the president decides he was wrong."

"Ride your motorcycle and the companion of others. Safety in numbers or just in case." "Why do you feel that way, Harold?" "Something he said about those boys transferring to other chapters. They may not feel the same way as the new president." "Got it, Harold, my bed awaits!" Heading upstairs. Reggie felt his brother was holding back. Maybe once he relaxed a bit.

Reggie also understood why they didn't want to have a war started in a small town cause the damage would be astronomical. Dressing for bed, Fluffy started to suddenly get tired. Maybe it was the warm milk. Reggie decided he would help with kid activities while parents went to the Valentine's Day event. Closing his eyes, he felt himself falling asleep.

Harold had evening talk with Hildi explaining the night's events. "I had to make a deal Hildi to keep our town safe. Oh Hildi, I wish you could have seen Miss Lilly riding that motorcycle. She is a woman of mystery! I miss you Hildi, good night.

As a cold wind started to beat against the side of the house. Harold slipped further into his down comforter to stay warm. Closing his eyes, he fell asleep fast. Another slap against the garage door. Startled but concerned, Harold grabbed his shotgun, heading for the garage. Turning on the lights, Harold checked the corners but noticed a piece of board was loose smacking against the garage wall. Using a couple of large nails to keep it from smacking the wall. Harold would never have been concerned about noise before. Thinking for a moment he knew his concerns were for Reggie.

Headed back to his room. He was wide awake, so he grabbed his briefcase, and started going through the calendar. Not many cases were pending for divorce, so that was a good omen. With three pregnancies all due around the same time, it is good, but we need more pregnancies. *Half our town needs to be expecting for our plan to work.* As the words on the paper became a blur, Harold was asleep in his bed with briefcase laid open next to him.

At 6:00 AM, Millie quietly started breakfast. Poached eggs seemed like a good idea over light toast with a slice of Turkey bacon on the side. Juice poured, coffee steaming and breakfast served. Walking to the stairwell she hollered, "Boys, breakfast!"

After a few minutes a very groggy man stumbled into the dining room. "Sir, did you have a problem last night?" "No, why would you ask?" Grabbing Harold by the hand and pulling him to the garage. Opening the side door Harold saw a mess. Confused, Harold looked around. Hearing a noise, Harold grabbed a bat and crouched as he looked around the back of his car to find a family of raccoons. The amounts of air that came from Harold's lungs showed he'd been scared.

Laughing from the doorway, Reggie announced, "Guess you showed them!" "Animals show up here because of you, they think you're their leader!" "Well, I am large, furry, and fluffy. So, it's not a big leap." "You could be the Papa raccoon! Plus, there's no food you won't eat!" "Not true, I don't like fried okra or fat back." "OK, well just two foods then."

"You boys get back into that house and eat your food. It's getting cold." Heading back to the table, plates were refilled and warm. "So, what's your plans for today, Reggie?" "I was thinking I would fix up on the garage, reorganize things." Harold smiled. "That would be helpful there, brother." "I noticed a few things that needed some attention. We still have an account at the hardware store?" "Yes, and one at the lumberyard. You need to use the truck?" "Yes, Harold, I need me some supplies." "Sounds like you have a busy day planned."

Reggie responded with, "I have a list of odd jobs to do." "I will let both places know you will be coming in for supplies." Getting dressed, Harold headed for his office. Reggie then grabbed his list for jobs and supplies. "Here I found you a hat from your farm workdays." "Thanks Millie, you are a Peach."

Heading to the hardware store first, he was greeted like a conquering hero who came home from the Wharf, lots of remembering days gone by. Next was the lumber mill, where Fluffy helped load trucks before he shopped for his supplies. Greg, who was the owner of the lumberyard, announced. "Hey man, wanna job?" "I would love to help you out when needed, but I need to do some fixing on our house. My brother knows the law, but not much about keeping up the house." "So, you volunteered Bud." "Of course I did, we are family."

Loading up the truck, Reggie said his farewell to all. Kal waved. "Put you down, ready for a game?" "I have some improvement projects." "The guys and I could give you a hand after school." "After school then." "Actually, we can't go on the field trip because we gave a nerdy a wedgie." "Oh, So you guys are in trouble." "But if we help you, we are trying to redeem ourselves." "OK, get your guys meet me at the house." "OK dude, thanks for saving my bacon." "Get busy Kal, before your mom finds you."

Kal came out with, "Mom is sick. It's hard not to get yelled at, Reggie" "Yes, it's a mom thing, you know, now get going," Reggie cracked. As Reggie drove home to start work and had the boys already beat him from town?

"Millie started us on organizing the garage." "Actually, that was a smart idea so we can find the right tools for the job." Putting hooks on a board with holes makes it easier to find against a white background. Each boy was assigned a box filled with tools. "So, all the 3/8 wrenches together, hammers, etcetera." "OK, we will have to back the automobiles out of the garage, for cleaning the floor."

"Now any tool that takes power we put here where it can be seen easily,

Saws and blades here, don't forget the guard, so no one loses a finger." As the garage showed improvement, Millie announced. "Lunch is served."

Standing next to the sink, was Millie, passing out soap and towels. "Lose those hats gentlemen. Men do not wear work hats to the table." "Yes ma'am." After filling lunch, they went back to work. The garage now looked well kept. Kal kept asking about the repairs. "What's on your mind Kal?" "Well, you know me and the other Cal are going to the prom, and we are trying to make some bucks for flowers and junk."

Laughing aloud, Reggie spoke. "Yeah, girls are a pain in ass like that." "Pictures, tuxedos, Chicks are expensive." Reggie agreed with those feelings. "So, I guess you boys want jobs?" "Yes, we need to make that money. So, do we pay for their dumb dress?" Thinking a moment, Reggie explained. "Your tuxes and her dress are supposed to match, and your boutonniere and her corsage are supposed to match. Also, no work boots. Replace them with dress shoes." "How do you have fun during the after party in a monkey suit?" Whined Kal. "It will be fine, And yes I will hire you boys."

"Like will my mom kiss me in front of my date?" "Probably on the cheek." "I'd rather go mudding instead, but the girls already said yes." "So, what do we fix first?" Looking at the walls, Reggie said. "We need to secure all those loose boards and find a home for my new friends." Car looked a bit confused. Cal 2 peeked in the box to find a family of raccoons. "The old cabin is abandoned again. Should be workable for the time being."

A long walk to bring the family to their new home. Reggie started looking at the cabin. Thinking *it would be great to rebuild it*. "I spent a lot of time here as a kid. It was my sanctuary. Even my father allowed me this small space to be my own." "I remember, he kept sour balls in a candy jar." Smiled Kal #1. "I can remember being so afraid of him."

"I know full grown men that feared his wrath." Smiled Reggie. As they walked down the wooded path, a blue Jay came through. "Early spring," smiled Reggie. Finishing with the loose forwards, "Next on the list was the shutters." "It's getting close to time for school to let out. Reggie, could we see your bike?" "I guess it wouldn't hurt." As he pulled back the cover, Kal gasped. "She is so pretty!" A deep sapphire blue with ape handlebars and shiny Chrome accents.

"Wow, mom and dad would never allow me to have one of these." "My parents were dead set against it. So as not to upset mom, I waited until they passed away before I bought this one." "So, what was it like to be in a club?"

Thinking about this answer, Reggie said, "You have to prospect for a year first before being considered to be a patched member, but you get a big family who promises to be with you no matter what happens." "So when you accept, there's just no leaving. Do you miss your brothers?" asked Kal. "To a degree I do miss them, but I have the best brother anyone could ask for."

Frank and Harold heard Reggie speech knowing he truly meant the advice he gave to the kids. "Kal, field trip what happened?" "We gave the nerdy A wedgie." "So now you will personally go to his home and apologize to both of his parents and their son also." "Yes, Sir." Heading to the car, Kal nodded to Reggie. "Frank, I gave our Kal one and two a job to pay for prom stuff." He tried to put the boys to use. "I see. The garage has never looked so good. You're a good man, Reggie." "I can help with the bowling alley parties while the adults are at their event." "Thanks, it will help parents a lot."

Harold looked around. "Not bad work." "Our lumber mill manager offered me a job loading trucks today. I told him to give me a call when he needed help!" "Helping with teenagers too.?" "Sometimes it's good to talk with an adult that isn't your parent." "So true," Harold fully admitted to being nervous when Dad called you into his study. "It seemed like Dad was always angry with us."

"He expected us to be perfect, just like him. He did come to law school graduation. He was expecting you to play Pro Football." "Well, I did too. The practice I put in, my grades weren't the problem." "I hate to admit this, but I was a bit homesick in college. People are not nice far from home."

Dinner was a combination of leftovers. Harold looked at Millie. "We do not waste food. Only foolish folks waste food." "You remind me of my mom." "I have been a part of your family for many years, Harold, and I know how she wanted her home to be kept. So, it will be done by her standards." Smiling Reggie was like, "what did I miss?" "Just reminiscing about your mom." "All right, leftovers! I love cold meatloaf sandwiches the next day." "Your dad loved them too, Reggie." "See Home is

Where Your Heart Is and the best food in the tri-county area."

"Thank you for the compliment, but I know there are better cooks than I." "But I'm starving, so could I fight a bear for dinner." "Sit down boys." There was light conversation about the day's events. Millie started with how clean and organize the garage is. Laughing, "Boys will do just about anything to avoid parents when they're thrown off the trip." "Where's your new family?" Asked Harold.

"I took them out to the old cabin. I was thinking about putting the cabin deck together," said Reggie. "It would be a good summer project for you." "Reggie, the kids will be looking for summer jobs. Cheap labor," smiled Harold. "Keeping them busy won't be difficult," cackled Reggie. "It also keeps them out of trouble. Money helps grease the wheels. Is Kal #1 going to college?" "Yes, I believe Frank and Roz mentioned it. They want him close by, but he wants to be far away." "Remember how pissed Dad was, because it was farther than 200 miles, so you needed to set up a dorm room?" "God, he ragged on me over that." "So maybe I'd be good at talking to the teens."

Smiling, Harold said, "Yes, I believe the kids would trust you. While their parents are busy with events." "So, I could help provide things for them to do." "Do you segregate girls?" asked Millie. "No, they can swing a hammer as good as their counterparts." "That's good." Millie smiles, "How do you feel about girls being in rifle club?"

"If they can hold their own against the guys, go for it." Millie nodded. "When I was growing up it was a triple whammy. Female, black, and can shoot better than every boy, so we were blackballed."

Harold then explained, "Most men from back in the day believe women were the fairer sex and were segregated to babies and housewife duties. Mom could shoot. Did you know that fluff?"

"No way." Harold walked over to the sideboard, reaching behind the mirror was her target. Perfect scores as Fluffy looked through each target. "Let me guess. Dad was not amused." "Hell no, he was majorly pissed off, but she never backed down." Millie spoke up. "She gave lessons so if we were home alone, they could handle what came through the door. Your mom started a women's club to prove their proficiency with all forms of dissent."

"During the wars, women picked up a gun, worked the fields and ran the household." "Your mom shot a turkey and made your dad Clean it. It was a bet, and Harold Senior lost. She never even went to the gun safety course, so her next bet was to get a buck, which she did. An 8-point buck, even though Sir was a bit pompous, He was proud of her buck, so he had it hung in his office."

"So, mom put the men in their place, then put on a dress to serve dinner. Nice. Our mom was a tough lady." "Your parents even had contests about grades in college." "Sounds like our mom, healthy competition." Heading out to the garage, Fluffy started his bike, checking its fluids. "She's perfect. So why are you looking at it sideways?"

"It was kept to nice, I don't believe it's over here." Harold looked at him, nodding. "That's why I suggested you stay in town. So, these projects needed to be done close by." Harold put his arm around his brother's shoulders. "So, think it will hold up both of us?" "Yeah. Why?" "Take me for a cruise before we crash for the night?" "Really? Cool. Here's gloves, jacket, and the helmet so your brain isn't road pizza." Heading out of town, cruising on the back roads.

As Millie watched them, she knew Harold would need someone to take his place if his heart quits on him. High cholesterol is nothing to play with. Smiling as they came back into view. "Damn it's cold riding it, but it was fun." Fluffy laughs, "Maybe we get you 1 to ride." "As weird as it seems, I believe I would like that very much." Invited Herald.

"You can help me with the cabin. You'll get a good workout." "It is a possibility. The events are every other weekend, so I could help you too." "Alright, you two. Hot chocolate and cookies and then bed." "Yes ma'am." "Boys, behave. I will see you in the morning, God willing," Millie whispered. "His test results are on your nightstand."

Harold went into the study to have his nightly discussion with Hildi. "Hildi, our boy, did a good job with the town boys. Talking about college programs and their aspirations. He'd have made a great counselor. Millie and I let him in on your prowess with a rifle boy. He was surprised, but things are starting to fall into place. Now to get the baby count up. I miss you Hildi. Goodnight." Shuffling up the stairs, Harold went to bed. And sleep came easily tonight.

As Fluffy got ready for bed. Getting comfortable, Fluffy grabbed for his glasses, an issue he didn't discuss. During a fight two guys jumped in and messed up his face so bad his eyesight was ruined. So, glasses were a necessary evil. Shaking his head, he grabbed

Harold's blood panels. *Seems he's been living a soft life here*. Reading Doc Halloway's notes, *he needs to lose 100 lbs. Dangerously high BP, high cholesterol*, so he changes diet. *Cutting down alcohol and cigars. Now I get why Millie overloaded us on vegetables instead of meat.*

After reading all reports, Fluffy knew he belonged here to help Harold. *This is it for me*. Slipping the papers in its folder. *I need to speak with doc in the morning*. Turning out the light sleep was elusive again. *Is my brother dying? Will all this help?* More questions rolled around in his mind. By the time he started to fall asleep, the sun had started to peak through the high clouds.

Dressing in layers for warmth, Fluffy decided he needed a tar coffee to keep him up today. Reggie was enjoying his coffee when Millie came walking in, looking at the coffee pot. She knew what was in it.

A substance that resembled coffee, but in all actuality was liquefied tar. It has a dual purpose, to drink, or cover the holes on the roof. “Heavens,” scolded Millie, turning off the machine. Then she dumped out the black sludge. Harold stood behind Millie, “Let me guess, he tried to make coffee.” “Don't worry Sir, I will have a new pot done fast.” “So, having a little trouble sleeping?” asked Harold. “Yes, my brain is not shutting off.”

“We have plenty of books to bore you to death.” “Let's be honest, books needed to be adventurous before I could get into them.” “I remember even history had to have bloody battles to hold her attention.” Laughing. “Remember our reenactment of wars?”

"Yes, and a month to clean up afterwards. Shit we got the pleasure of cleaning everyone's lawn. Dad was good for those kinds of lessons. At our expense." "Hey, if you are repairing the shutters today, maybe wear your glasses for measurements." "But how?" I was notified of your needing to go to the hospital." "So, you never said anything?" "I figured you would tell me when you were ready."

"Gotta be honest, these are some ugly glasses. I got you an appointment with my guy. Glasses made there on the premises. Maybe find a style that won't make you feel self-conscious." "Yeah, they told me the damage was severe, so I was a candidate for contacts. But now wire frames are the same price as birth control glasses." "Lilly will take you over tomorrow. I will be at the event to supervise. Friday night through Sunday morning for church. The projects for the kids would be helpful. Plus, Reverend Thomas will be starting to prepare for the Easter program."

"Got it. Evenings Frank and Rose let the kids have their own bowling party. You know, pizza and wings, etcetera. So maybe you could supervise. Otherwise, it's Reverend Thomas. No one truly wants that. Maybe encourage the behavior of parents coming home to clean house."

"It makes home more appealing when mom and dad don't have chores when they arrive home, keeping the good mojo going." "Exactly Fluffy, you will be an asset." "So, am I excused, Dad? I have supplies to purchase." "So, when it's warmer, I think we should repaint the house with shutters, a lighter shade or white." "Are you doing the painting?" "If need be, but now they have spray painter gadgets." "That is true, but quality is important."

"To be continued." Grabbing the truck keys, Fluffy headed out to see Doc Halloway. Arriving to Greeting from Nurse Kelly. "You look much better." "Thanks, It helps when you aren't getting punched in the face daily." "Exactly," Squeals Doc Halloway. "So, let's talk in my office. OK, Reggie, you sounded upset on the phone last night."

"I know legally you can't tell me about Harold, but Christ, is he gonna die on me?" "Eventually we all are gonna die, Fluff." "It is true, but his tests were a bit concerning." "However, after a bit of arm twisting, he agreed to cooperate with some adjustments. Not major ones though. It starts with two cups of caffeine, then green tea for the rest of the day. Brandy twice per week and two cigars a week. He follows the diet. He needs exercise though." Leave that to me Doc. I even had Him on my bike last night." "Shit, I'd have paid money to see Harold on a sled."

"I got the kids helping me with some work. Harold had let go for a while, started with cleaning the garage. Today there are shutters, but eventually we are going to redo the old cabin together. Plenty of walking without the title of exercise."

"Millie keeps an eye on him, but I think he will need some encouragement." "Plus, I am on the kid's entertainment committee." Laughing hard, Doc said, "Well, you have always literally been a one-man wrecking crew." "Not in many years, but thanks for the vote of confidence. Later I got some shutters to fix up, even got Harold to think about repainting the house."

"Wow Fluffy, you are on a serious roll. I believe he's gotten too complacent, not trying to improve his station. He needs to start living again." Doc spoke softly, "I agree with you. Lilly tries to keep him motivated." "Shit maybe if my brother got laid, He wouldn't be so damn cantankerous." "At least, it's considered cardio exercise," smiled Doc Halloway. "I'm ready to find him a professional girlfriend!"

As Reggie left, he started going over his repair list. Knowing he could at least get the first-floor shutters done, picking up new hinges and a paint scraper. Arriving home, Reggie unloaded the truck, pulling out a short ladder first, taking down each shutter with care. Scraping off the loose paint was a balmy 50° Kal #1 arrived. "I am grounded. From fun activities. So, where do I start?" "As I take them down, they need scraping down for new paint."

Before long Kal's friends arrived, forming an assembly line. Scrap, then use the air hose to get rid of dust. Before the spray-painting equipment came out. "The bottom floor had 10 windows. If all goes well, the second floor will be finished by Saturday."

Looking over the paint on the House itself, it was not as bad as Reggie figured it would be. Planning how the paint needs to be. Thinking for a moment, *stain would be sucked into the wood. Note to self; ask Harold, which he prefers.* Millie announced lunch was served. After stuffing themselves, Reggie announced, "Time to put back the shutters." Millie asks, "Boys, I will see you tomorrow?"

Kal nods, "Sure thing Miss Millie, hanging out with you is better than babysitting." "Make sure you do all the homework because I am in charge of that party at the bowling alley." "Really?" Yelled Cal #2. "Yes, So don't make me out to be a clown."

Heading out, the boys gave a salute to Reggie. As Harold pulled in, he noticed the shutters. "That's a really good job! So, how much do I owe the kids?" Reggie said, "They will work on the 2nd floor shutters, 65° tomorrow!" "Not to dampen your excitement, but how are you planning on getting to the attic shutter?"

"Damn, now I have to think about it." Opening his list, he asked, "Oil based paint or stain?" "Why?" "Apparently someone had the color refreshed." "Yes, it's a hybrid type of color." "Well, what's the name of the color? Did you get it locally?" "Let me check my paperwork for the color we used." Millie yelled, "Wash up for supper." Reminding him, "You have a meeting tonight." Yes, of course, I need to approve the final preparation. So, you got the pizza for the bowling party?"

"Yes Sir. League is on Friday night, and the party is Saturday. Home Sunday morning for church. I got it, Harold." "Just checking because the Reverend Thomas." "I can handle him brother, that Easter parade & spring pageant." "So, the ones who already are pregnant are just there. Just like any other member would be." "OK. Just checking because Judith is a bit jumpy." "She was all for this plan until she was one of the first ones with a child. Now she has reservations because her political career is starting to heat up." "So, will she keep this surprise bundle of joy? I heard she already asked about other options."

"Yes, I believe there's a counseling session scheduled with her and her husband, Jack." "Who's lucky #3?" "Lisa and Lawrence Sykes. She's excited because they've been trying for a while. Larry isn't thrilled." "Guess she had to put more men on the job," Laugh Reggie, shaking his head.

"I went to the post office to have my correspondence sent here, but he handed me a whole box of mail that had been keeping until I got out." "Well, there's no keeping you quiet about where you reside." "Harold, if I act scared, then they've won." "No intimidation here. Plus, President signed a document that's an honor code violation. They believe in their rules no matter what else happens. A club member gives you his word it's like gold to them." "I understand, same code soldiers have." "yes, the same valor expected by soldiers. Bikers had a code also. They will ride for charities. They are the biggest donors for Christmas. As big and burly as most are, a sick child will melt their heart."

"So, I will tell you it angers me to hear things like old dirty bikers because so many instances it's just not true." Millie yelled, "Eat your dinner Cold! I am going home!" "Whoops. We're sorry Millie." Looking at Reggie, Millie announced, "Minnie Sue will come back tomorrow as housekeeper." "Oh, no more of your cooking?" whined Reggie. "No, you are not that lucky. I will be here to help. As her baby is 8 weeks old and she maybe could be called home for the baby." Nodding in agreement, "Harold suggested Minni Sue works half days for a month until she's ready to commit to full time again. The best of both worlds."

"Harold, we can always count on you to do the right thing." "Yes indeed.

That's why I am so good at my job." "Even as a lawyer, you were known for being honest and fair no matter the case." "Now go home to your kids, we can clean up the kitchen." "Reggie, could you please make sure those boys don't leave nails in the lawn. Barefoot season will be here soon enough."

"On it Miss Millie!" "Also, rinsed off the dishes before putting them in the dishwasher. I will start them in the morning." Harold growled, "I run a dishwasher!" Laughing at that proposal, "I have pictures from the last time. No thanks, it took me 3 days to clean up the mess." "How did he do that?" Asked Reggie. "Too much bourbon and no common sense. Started the blender without the top being secured." "Oops!" cracked Harold.

"I should have made you clean it up with a hangover. You wouldn't do it again. For a while." "Touché Millie, I learned my lesson. No more drunk milkshakes." "See, my Big Brother isn't always perfect!" "Shut up little brother, or I will start listing your faults."

"I get it!" "Hurry up and check for nails. We got a kitchen before this meeting." "In other words, I get to clean the kitchen while you go over preparations for your Valentine's Day event."

"So, I would guess aphrodisiacs are a must." "Lilly usually provides adult treats." "OK, did anyone account for allergies?" "Doc gave everyone a physical and asked about allergies." "So, you covered that. Just asking so no one dies from anaphylactic shock. I have seen that and it's not pretty."

"OK, I will head out to my meeting then." Reggie spoke. "I would be honored to clean up the kitchen for you, Maza!" "Knock it off, Reggie." "Shall I shine your shoes to Maza?" A right-hand smack was felt, "I said stop, Reggie!" "Boy old age has made you cranky, Big Brother." Harold left showing his aggravation by burning rubber.

Cleaning the kitchen to Milli's satisfaction was kind of fun. Looking through the library until he came across Mark Twain stories. That always piqued his interest of adventure. Settling in bed with a book, warm milk and ginger snaps as the pages fell away, Reggie's eyes fluttered as he fell asleep. Harold moved Reggie's empty glass away from the edge of the nightstand. Heading to his study. He spoke to Hildi about the event. "Reggie is still a smart ass, but he seems to be fitting in with the teens."

"Someone helping with the teens is a good thing. He even has his own work crew. These boys need money for prom, so it effectively works out. They like working For Reggie, maybe it's because he's a kid at heart. Tomorrow, Lilly is taking Reggie to get a decent pair of glasses. Prison gave him birth control glasses. But that's all for tonight. I love you and miss you."

Heading off to bed he noticed Reggie had been in the library smiling at the fact Reggie was reading. "Who knew you could read brother?" Pleased set Reggie's accomplishments. He knew one day Reggie would be ready to take his place, for running the town. Then he will rest in peace. "I can't go yet. Reggie needs some training on the town budgets and such." Herald's shoulders started to relax, climbing into bed, a tiny pill he'd been taking even before his blood panel was checked. Unbeknownst to the town Herald had gone to an unspecified hospital to put stents in his heart.

Dale, Doc Halloway, was sworn to secrecy, even Lilly doesn't know, but probably suspects that his heart is full of cholesterol. So, is taking this little pill going to fix it? Not really, but it will buy Herald some time to get everything in place for Reggie to take over. Maybe have a wife and children. Falling asleep, Harold dreamt of him and Hildi walking around the town on warm summer nights. An image came into view of Reggie coaching a baseball team with a fair-haired woman with four girls.

Looking into Harold's eyes Hildi whispers, "Reggie was the best decision. Now our town is blossoming again. We have many new babies in the town. This is more than what we could hope for. Doc

Halloway is running a training clinic for midwives!"

Harold slept well. He knew his plans would have merit for this town. Millie knocked softly, "Sir, It's time to get up." "Where's Reggie?" "It's 8:00 AM. Miss Lilly took him to his appointment. He said he will start on the 2nd floor shutters when he comes back. Duwanna said you have no appointments except for the weekends event so you can sleep in. Maybe help Reggie with those shutters?"

"That's a fine idea. I don't normally get to play hooky." Having breakfast, Harold found a flannel shirt and jeans. "Wow Sir, I've never really seen you do a casual day." Heading out to the garage, Harold looked at Reggie's list. Hauling out the large ladder and started preparing to take off the shutters. Call #1 and Calvin arrived and started snickering. "Uh Oh Judge needs some help."

"Yes, gentlemen, show me how Reggie had all of this set up please." Before they completed the prep, Reggie arrived home. Lilly jumped out of the truck. "Now Harold, how about you come have coffee with me while these boys start work?" "Oh, that sounds fine. So, your appointment?" Pulling out a pretty new pair of wireframes. "He got a second pair for free for let the ophthalmologist students give him an examination. These girls were beautiful." Cooed Lilly.

Reggie snickered. "I'm all about the education, Lilly." "Oh, I am sure you are Fluffy!" Shaking his head, Harold headed in for coffee. Once inside Reggie's smile reappeared. "Let's do this assembly line again. It seemed to be efficient." After the shutters were down, they followed the same instructions as the day before. Once all were put back, Calvin and Cal asked about the attic shutter. "OK, I'm on the ladder!" calling to Calvin and Kal inside, up in the attic. After loosening, the shutter came down.

Once on the ground, Calvin cleaned it up. Passing up the shutter, Reggie stood on the roof and Harold went at it from the inside. Once it was being held in place, Reggie attached the new hardware. Kal and Calvin stood on the roof with pride. "OK boys, clean up duty. No nails on the lawn." Once the lawn was inspected, Harold called them into the house. "Yes, Sir." "So who are we paying?" Hands went up. "Me Sir!" "Let me confer with my road boss." Smiling and nodding, Harold enjoyed messing with them.

"So, $20 each sound reasonable." "Yes, Sir." But little Rosie spoke up, "Reggie, should be paid too. He works hard, Judge Harold." The serious expression on her face told Harold she truly believed Reggie was like one of the boys. Roz announced, "I am here to pick up my children." Passing out envelopes to each child made them feel special. As Cal and Calvin passed Reggie, he stuck an extra 20 in their shirt pockets with a wink. Roz thanks Reggie for giving the boys a job. "They listened, took direction and were a delight to work with. We will have more work next week provided the weather holds out."

As parents prepared to leave for the weekend, children were getting this speech about behavior and fighting with their siblings. Rosie, little Rose Marie, showed her exasperation. "Tell them there are no scary movies, I need sleep. I get to help Reverend Thomas with our Easter Parade." Calvin and Cal both acknowledged that it is an important job. Winking at Cal and Calvin pulled out ET to watch tonight. Rose exploded with, "Calvin, You can sit next to me!" "Well, that is such a privilege." "Besides, you like snacks too!" "That I sure do and I bet you like candy!" smiled Calvin.

"Here, put this in your pig." "Wow, $5 for me?" "Yes, you are a big help around here." As Roz and Frank heard the conversation, they truly knew the kids would be alright in this town. Preparing for Valentine's event, but Roz was hoping she could just hang out with Frank. She was feeling ill and just wanted her man to cuddle with. An overnight bag was packed, calling out instructions Cal and Calvin were in charge.

"Oh boy, this will be interesting." Maybe we should talk to Harold about this weekend. I'm sure he knows how sick. I have been. Remember to drop off the girls for Easter choir practice. Then head out to help Reggie. So, will you be helping cover your tux?" "I have to wait until my date chooses a color, so my buttoner matches her flowers." "Wow, who talked to you about prom etiquette?" "Reggie did." "Sounds like he is a good influence." "Mah, can I be honest with you?"

"Always, son." "Right, well, Harold tried to help and excuse my mouth, but ma, he looked almost Gray. Before I could check him out, Lilly took him in for coffee." "Thank you for bringing this to our attention." "Like he is harder on us, but for being old He's alright." Franks spoke, "Does that mean there's hope for all of us old folks?"

"Maybe, We will have to see your report card!" Cracked Kal and Calvin. "Sounds familiar," boys laughing. "You better get going before we increase our rate." "Don't push your luck, gentlemen." "Get outta here, parental units." Passing out hugs 2 smaller children. "Be good for your brother. There's a movie and snacks so have fun."

Heading to the car, Roz started thinking about Harold's health. "Could he know he won't be around much longer?" Driving to the Beaver Inn, something wasn't sitting right. "Harold and Lilly are already here." Once they signed in to register, Frank asked to speak with Harold. "So, what's going on, What's on your mind?"

Frank asks, "Could Roz and I stay together? She's still sick. Can't keep much down except that Coke syrup stuff from the doc." Lilly spoke from behind Harold's shoulder. "We understand. Lisa is here with Lawrence. But where is Judith?" "I don't know. She's been staying out of sight."

"There's no other option for our town. Sounds like Doc Halloway will need to keep an eye on Judith." As the tables were filled with goodies. Lilly made sure plenty of crackers were available for sick tummies, but in each guest room there was a basket of personal goodies. Toys, edible undies, etcetera, feathers and a crop. "It will be interesting when they all done Cupid outfits. Ladies will be in Lingerie. Morning sex is always a good way to start the day."

As the club members arrive, a hum starts to begin, as everyone starts mingling. At midnight Lilly began the key grabs, sending Roz and Frank to their room first. Judith arrived late with a green tint to her face. Harold whispers, "I see that bug got you too?" "Jesus, I feel like Death warmed over, just stopped fighting it. I was hoping to get some of that Coke syrup from the doc." Walking over to the desk, he picked up a phone receiver. Harold dialed up the doc. "We have another one in need of that magical

Luxor." laughing aloud, Dale said. "Open a can of coke and let it go flat."

"The syrup comes up, but the pharmacist could offer help." "No, she isn't ready for a public announcement." "OK, I will make sure that Don has some pints available. She isn't handling this well at all." Finishing his clean up, Reggie decided he should check on the boys. After making a sandwich. Reggie sat in the recliner putting on his new specs. He looked through Harold's Rolodex to find the number, Reggie called. A male voice answered. "Are you Kal or Celvin?" He laughed, "I'm Calvin, I brought the entertainment." "Oh. Lord," whined Reggie. "I brought ET. Rose Marie doesn't like scary movies."

"I see," said Reggie. "I figured I would check in. I'll see you boys in the morning." "Right after we dropped the girls off. Dad pulled out stuff for our party at the bowling alley." "We will start working at 9:00 AM. That gives us time for breakfast." "So true," Cal stated. "Coffee is life, just ask my parents." "Yes, but adults are always running behind so the need copious amounts of the bean juice. You work all day, it keeps us studios boys from falling asleep in history class." "OK, see you in the morning. Goodnight boys."

As Reggie finished his second sandwich the phone rang, it was Doc Halloway. "Can I drop in to see you?" "Sure, I am available." "I am heading over." Click.

Just then the phone rang again. This time it was Reverend Thomas. "I would like to chat with you. I closed the rectory at about 10:00 PM, so I will arrive at about 10:30. Is that acceptable?" "Yes, Reverend, that will be fine." Cleaning up the kitchen, so Minni Sue won't have a mess in the morning.

Headlights flashed in the kitchen window. Reggie greeted him at the door. "Nice work on the garage." "The kids were a real great help. How may I help you, Dale?" "I have to deliver these to Harold, put them in his room. Not curious?" "Of course I am, but Harold has always been a private person. However, if I had to guess. Nitro for his heart?" "Damn you knew?" "Dale, I can tell when he's in trouble. But at this point, he isn't ready to tell me. I figured when he personally came to escort me from prison, there was more to it. I have it under control, but the folks of this town depend on him to solve the most basic of problems."

"The fact you noticed that repairs were not getting done. So, long as you understand." "So, how long has he been taking Nitro?" "About two years, give or take. My advice, you do the heavy lifting, let him help, but with small jobs. The reasoning behind it? He stopped taking care of himself when Hildi passed away." "So, if it weren't for Minni Sue, Millie, or Janet, we'd have found him dead a while ago." "Those ladies keep him on the straight and narrow. Duwanna handles the office like a pro." "Keeping him on his diet will be tough. So how are you feeling?" "Fine, It's amazing what decent food and exercise will do for you."

"Go ahead and put his pills where they go. I will pretend not to know about his heart." Dale left, but the conversation left a dark hole in his heart concerning Harold. Just as he walked back to the recliner, the front hall bell rang, signaling the arrival of Reverend Thomas. Allowing Reggie to look into his eyes, which was necessary when signing up at sizing up your opponent. "So, what brings you to see a heathen like me?"

"I guess we got off to the wrong foot?" "So start over?" "OK, agreed Reggie." "What do you need, Reverend Thomas?" "You seem to have a way with the teen crowd." "I do?" questioned Reggie laughing. "Yes, they don't normally agree to manual labor." "OK, I put them to work because they discovered prom equal lots of spending money. Matching flowers and clothes. So, I explained prom etiquette. The after party is a mom and dad decision."

"Sounds like you gave solid information to the teens. Parents seem to appreciate your style." "Look, Reverend Thomas, I am exactly the very same as I was in high school, except I am heavier than I was back then. The scars I have come from never backing down from a bully, or protection of someone else." The Reverend nodding in agreement. "I do have some concerns regarding Harold."

"Let's hear them, Padre." "His complexion has almost a gray tone to it." Letting out a deep breath, Reggie started with, "A.) He works in a dusty office. B.) He doesn't spend much time outside where the sun gives you vitamin D. He has high blood pressure and cholesterol, and his job is stressful. That's all he does for this town and its people. Give Harold some slack. He works hard."

"Will you be here to help Harold?" "Yes, Reverend Thomas, I will be here. So, if you will excuse me, teenagers at 9:00 AM to start work." "Goodnight." As Reverend Thomas pulled out of the driveway, all the hair stood up on the back of Reggie's neck. Knowing that Padre liked to start shit, he wondered what was coming. Heading to bed with warm milk and a stash of cookies after his snack, concern got the best of him. Sneaking a peek into this medicine, thinking to himself. Cholesterol, BP meds and Nitro. *Sounds like his heart is about to take a powder if we don't get him in shape with less stress. Shit, this is going to be a mess. I wonder how much Miss Lilly knows*, Heading back to bed. Sleep will be elusive again tonight.

Back at the Beaver, things were progressing nicely. Lots of noise coming from rooms. “Harold, are you looking for me?” cooed Lilly. “Well, I assume you would get questions about gift baskets.” “Some had questions. I provided visual aids to help them along. So, are you ready for your lesson?” “Always when it comes to you, Miss Lilly.” Lilly smiled. “I truly enjoy our lessons, but we will go at a slower pace. I don't need to be calling Doc Hallaway, do I?” “No, I see too much of him as it is.”

Walking into Lilly's room, closing the door, he felt a sense of relief. No expectations, just enjoying each other's company. Lilly treated Harold with kid gloves. Lilly was entrusted with the true extent of Harold's health issues. So, with loving, gentle arms, Lilly helps him unwind. Because of her previous husband's, Lilly learned it was necessary to keep a medicine bag prepared. She took classes to be able to perform CPR, Breath sounds, and pulse. Lilly always came prepared for anything.

After some foreplay, Lilly let Harold rest for a few minutes, then gently brought him to heights of pleasure with a great ending. Lilly could also be counted on for a wonderful date. “I should get back to my room, people will gossip.” “So let them Harold, you need to say screw it, and no more holding the stress in.” Finally, Lilly yelled, “You fucking moron. I love you, Harold!”

"Wow, Lilly, that's the first time I ever heard you swear before." "Well, it got your attention, right?" Hugging her tight, he knew she meant every bit of it. Heading back to his room he felt he needed to tell Hildi. As he tucked himself into bed whispering, "Hildi I have forsaken you again. I love you Hildi, but tonight Miss Lilly told me. I was a moron, she loved me. I am confused. I love you, but I feel special love for her too. Is this wrong?"

Suddenly, a puff of warm air enveloped him. "I never wanted you to be lonely because you let me go. Enjoy your love with Lilly. I approve. It's OK." Going to sleep, Harold did not hear the others wake up for breakfast. As the noises drifted upward, Harold jumped up. Wearing a smoking jacket, he headed to the dining room. Busy people asked, "So, skiing or building a snowman?" "Guess what? These guys have a bowling alley and a roller-skating rink! Plus, an indoor pool!" "So, let's decide who's doing what." Passing out swimsuits, the Water warm to the help of nausea. Ladies trying to roller skate was a riot. Falling hurt a lot more than it used to on the old tailbone. Last before dinner would be bowling. Some ladies needed a nap. Even the men needed rejuvenation, with tables of snacks. Dinner would be served soon.

Back at the town, Reggie had accomplished much. Lots of color for the house itself. "So, guys go home, check on the little ones, then we will set up the bowling alley." "There are little kid games in the clown room so we can let Reverend Thomas babysit them." Smiling, Reggie agreed. "So, the kids started to ask what time." "If house chores are done, we start at 7:00 PM. Break!" Cal made sure his sisters did their chores.

Rose Marie asked, “Do we get to go to?” Smiling he says, “Yes.” “Oh wow we get the party too!” “Yes, hurry and clean your room.” Kal’s sister. Kate looked at her brother. “What's up?” “Kids have their own game room and Reverend Thomas can babysit.” “Oh, that's evil, but I love it.” “Can you bring her over? I need to help set up. Reggie's first time so I figured I should educate him.” “OK, but Rose Marie needs a bath. Must be those robes we're musty.” “I'll leave you to that.”

Kate was on the phone, making plans with her friends, yelling at her sister. “I ran you a bubble bath, so you smell better.” “You need a bath too!” “OK, I agree. I smell bad, so hurry up Shorty.” Kate was beginning pummeled with water. “Stop it, mom will be pissed. You know how she is about a clean dry bathroom.” “I was just having fun.”

"Touche Rose Marie. Here's your clothes, get me the brush and I will braid your hair, OK?" Kate took a shower too after cleaning up the bathroom. As Kate's friend started to arrive, Rose Marie was confused, announcing, "I get to go too this time!" Kate nodded in compliance. While makeup and hair spray were being used, Kate's friends asked about her little sister.

"Little kids are going to be in the clown room with Reverend Thomas as their babysitter." "Nice idea." "My brother does have his moments of usefulness." Dressing for success or to get asked to prom was the ultimate success. Suddenly Reverend Thomas arrived hitting the horn. Kate took her sister to the church van. "We are walking over, but it's too cold for Rose Marie." Peeking in the back, all the occupants were the little kids. Kate ran back into the house to look it over and lock it up.

Keys in hand Kate ran to join her friends. As they arrived, they heard music, lights flashing. Reverend Thomas was getting an earful about the clown room. Volunteers took turns with the little ones. Reggie greeted all the kids with smiles. Snacks were brought out, filling the tables and the lanes were ready. The jukebox cranked up. Reggie had gone into the back so it could be played without coins/

While at the Beaver Inn a band was a mixture of 50s to 70s music. Which usually brought a crowd to the dance floor. Just then some requests for disco music. Lilly thoroughly enjoyed the men trying to be cool with dancing. Lilly grabbed Harold's hand and asked for jitterbug music. Those 50s dances were always fun to try to recreate.

Frank truly tried to imitate the Night Fever dances. Harold chuckled. “These men are going to be sore tomorrow!” “They ideally will be loosened up for their more fun adventures.” “Oh, they will be ashamed in church guaranteed!” bitched Lilly. “The fruits of our labor should be noticed soon enough.” The evening started to wind down in the same fashion facing front and grabbing a set of keys. From the sounds in the hallway most people settled for a fast and functional lay.

All that activity tuckers out even the most macho man. Harold asked Lilly, “Would you mind if we watched a movie and cuddled and talked for a while?” “Why Yes, Harold, that will be fine.” “I need to share something with you. I spoke with Hildi last night.” “Harold, I do know you speak with her daily. I wanted her to know you love me too.” “It's OK for you to care for me until I go to meet her." "It means so much to me that you would bring it to Hildi." smiling.

"Hildi used to wear my shirts in college. Now you are wearing the same one she always favored. Here it goes. I am not as healthy as that, Halloway says. I had a heart attack and was taken to the hospital 3 towns away. I have stints, BP meds and Nitro." Thinking for a moment, Lilly smiled. "Not the first time I've heard this speech, Herald." "I felt if we were to have a relationship, you should know what you're getting into." "Well, truthfully, I have known since it happened, but I felt you would entrust me with these facts when you were ready. So that's the reason behind Reggie coming home?" "No, not exactly but the town folks tend to trust Reggie. If I had to step down to part time, he could help."

"So, Harold when will you tell him?" "Not quite prepared yet. I want to see how he does with teenagers first. If all goes well, then I will think about telling him." "OK, so how do we handle our relationship in public?" "The same as we normally do. They will gossip, but they will acclimate to what we ever we say." "So, are we going steady, no class ring?" Chuckled Lilly. "No, but you have my home and office keys." "That is true, Harold." Lilly peeked over at Harold, sleeping soundly, and slips out of bed. Lilly headed back to her own room, packing up.

Lilly knew people would be leaving to make it home for church. Roz and Frank were the first to leave, praying the bowling alley didn't get trashed. Judith and Jack left early also. Lisa and Lawrence decided on breakfast first. Breakfast buffets started at 6:00 AM until

11 AM. The rest started ambling towards the stairs, filling up for the ride home. The silence was deafening. Couples had to go home to their children and their mundane life.

But for two days, they were free to explore a side of them that has been in the shade for many years. Resentment had stopped for the most part. As people left and the parking lot emptied, there was a sadness. Lilly and Harold drove home together in case Harold got uncomfortable with spilling the beans. "So how do you feel this event did?" Ask Harold. "Judge Harold, I believe we will have more pregnancies." "Hopefully your optimism is accurate." "So how do you think Reggie did?" asked Lilly.

"I am sure he rose to the occasion, but he's not great at cleaning up." Dropping Lilly off at home, Harold decided to check out the bowling alley.

As Harold used the side door for receiving, he noticed a noise. Walking around with fists balled and ready for a fight. Frank came out of the kitchen. "So how did Reggie do?" "My kitchen was clean GI style. It shined, hand polished. I gotta admit I was pretty damn impressed," quipped Frank. "Do I expect a visit from Reverend Thomas?" Laughing hard, Frank Yelled. "They made Reverend Thomas the babysitter for the little kids!"

Giggling like a kid, Harold Whisper. "I bet he really enjoyed that. No gawking at the girls of high school. So, are you headed to church?" "I should check with Reggie, I'm sure he will want to finish refreshing the house color. Plus, almost 70° today. It will be a working outside day." Pulling in, Harold crept into the side door so as not to disturb Fluffy. To his surprise, his brother was cooking breakfast in a spotless kitchen. "Minni

Sue was sent home to spend Sunday with her family." Explained Reggie. "So, what is all this about?" "Let's just say enjoy a meal together." "OK little brother, what did you do and how much will this screw up cost me?"

"I am hurt, Harold. I am happy." "So do we play 20 questions here?" "No, I just want you to relax." Shaking his head. "OK, no more bullshit. What's up?" "I was going to ask you the same question." Thinking a minute. "So, what You know about my meds?" "Yes, and the small heart attack, so I'm in charge of exercise and doing the house renovations." "Alright, I will give you a chance at holding the reins." "No, not take over, but to help free up your time."

"Wow maybe I will get to work on Moms Flower Garden. All the windows need cleaning too. Once the weather stabilizes, we will bring out the gazebo setup” “Even though you are a hard ass I love you big brother.” “Right back atcha, little brother” “So church today, Big Brother?” “No, let's just work on the House. Racing is on the TV later. Let's eat, I need coffee.” growled Herald. While eating, Reggie gave the lowdown on last night's teen party.

Listening, Harold realized it was just good clean fun. “So, Frank was impressed with how clean his kitchen was.” “Incentives bring better workers.” “Ah, I get it, Bribery. Well, I gave the guys a speech about once parents learn you can be trusted, the restraint starts to come off.” “Jail philosophy?” “No, but that is part of their incentive program which includes freebie from the store.”

Thinking about the logic behind it. “So, if you teach them hard work brings them what they desire, they will try hard to achieve the ultimate goal. Cash is the name of the game." Laughing, Harold just nodded. "Maybe we should put you in charge. You seem to work rather well with the kids." "Better than I expected I have to admit." "We are a team, Harold. Now get your work clothes on, I never said I wouldn't put you to work." Cackled Reggie.

Pulling the outdoor furniture out Harold began using the soap to take off the access dirt and hose off the paint. Reggie had been working on the exterior of the house. Kal and Calvin arrived on scene. "So, what do we owe this surprise?" "Mom is letting us cut church because of how clean everything was when they got home." "So how about cleaning up the yard?" "OK what's the judge up to?" "He's washing off the furniture for the gazebo." "He looked pale." said Calvin. "I will take over for him"

As Calvin suggested he took over. Lilly pulled in. “So, what's up boys?” “Just helping the judge.” Rolling her eyes, she knew what they meant. Harold looked at the basket. “Picnic supplies?” “Yes, I figured the weather was good.” “Great idea.” “So, did you have some breakfast, or at least coffee?” Smiling with pride Herald announced, “Reggie made me breakfast.” “Who died?” asked Lilly.

“No one. I did it because I wanted to. Let's get you in the house.” “Why?” “So we can help you get hydrated. You look pale.” “It must be the sun.” “I will make some Lemonade.” “Sounds good, I'm sure the guys could use some too.” Lilly passed around glasses of lemonade. “Doc Halloway has some interesting findings.” “Really do tell.” “Seems the flu camouflaged the pregnancy symptoms. There are actually 3 pregnancies confirmed. So, the flu Is winding down a bit." "The Padre will have more to say."

"So what else is new?" "Nothing. He is getting a group going about moral decency." Shaking his head. "That damn foolish man has skeletons in his closet too." "It's also maybe the reason he keeps getting moved around to different postings." "After speaking with the doctor, he said that 6 now that we know about."

"He will call them in for a recheck and tell them," smiling Harold felt secure in this plan, but he may not survive to see the end of their census issues.

Epilog

As spring approaches, the pregnancy rates start to climb. However, Judge Harold needs to see his plan come to fruition. As his health declined, in his heart, he knew that he would need Reggie to carry out his plan. As Lilly spends more time caring for Judge Harold.

www.ingramcontent.com/pod-product-compliance
Lightning Source LLC
LaVergne TN
LVHW091141080826
845145LV00008B/2218

9781952497063